SHOWDOWN AT RED ROCK
THE CROCKETTS' WESTERN SAGA: 6

ROBERT VAUGHAN

WOLFPACK
PUBLISHING
— EST 2013 —

WOLFPACK
PUBLISHING
— EST 2013 —

Paperback Edition
Copyright © 2021 (As Revised) Robert Vaughan

Published in the United States by Wolfpack Publishing, Las Vegas

Wolfpack Publishing
5130 S. Fort Apache Road, 215-380
Las Vegas, NV 89148

wolfpackpublishing.com

Paperback ISBN 978-1-64734-787-1
eBook ISBN 978-1-64734-786-4

SHOWDOWN AT RED ROCK

Chapter One

A hot, dry wind moved through the canyon, pushing before it a billowing puff of red dust. The cloud of dust lifted high and spread out wide, making it look as if there were blood on the sun.

Will and Gid Crockett were headed for the town of Afton, where, they had been told, they would find a woman named Cat Clay.

"She was taken from me, against her will, by some outlaws," Peter Blaylock told them. "For a long time I didn't know where she was, but I just heard from a fella who says that he saw her workin' in a saloon over in Afton. I'll give you boys two hundred and fifty dollars apiece to go over there and get her. Fifty dollars now... and the rest when you bring her to me."

"You say she's working in a saloon?" Will asked.

"Yep."

"If that's the case, she's probably not being held against her will."

Peter shook his head. "No, I don't reckon she is," he admitted. "Not now anyway. But the thing is, I figure that over the last year...that's how long it's been since she was taken...she's probably had to do some things she's not proud of, you know, to stay alive. I reckon she thinks I won't be a' wantin' her any more. Only, that's not true. I want you to tell her that. And tell her that, no matter what she's had to do, I forgive her."

"What if she doesn't want to come back?"

"Then I want you to bring her back anyway. That's what I'm payin' you boys for."

"You might be forgiving her," Will said. "But if we bring her back by force...she may not be all that forgiving of you."

"You just take your money and do your job. I'll worry about that."

"All right, give us the money. If she hates your guts when we bring her back, it's no skin off our noses," Will said.

Normally, neither Will nor Gid would give a hoot in hell about Peter Blaylock's love life. But the two hundred fifty dollars apiece he offered them came at just the right time. The brothers were down to their last few dollars, so despite their initial dislike of the slimy little man who hired them, they accepted the job.

They had started on their journey the day before and, after two days of hard riding, were figuring to make Afton before nightfall.

"Hey, Will," Gid called out, shortly after they rode into the canyon. "Hold up a minute, will you? I gotta take a leak."

It was a peaceful moment. Will got off to adjust the cinch on his saddle while Gid tried to direct his stream to knock a fly off a mesquite branch.

The peace was shattered when Will heard a bullet pop by his ear, then ricochet off a nearby rock to fill the little canyon with its whine.

"Son of a bitch! Someone's shooting at us!" Will shouted.

Will and Gid Crockett had been under fire many times before...beginning with their days of riding with Quantrill during the Civil War. Because of their experience, they didn't have to waste time asking what was going on, nor looking at each other in confusion. They knew exactly what was going on, and they knew what to do about it. Simultaneously, they pulled their rifles out of the saddle sheaths while slapping their horses on the rump to send them out of the line of fire.

"He's up there," Will said, pointing to the top of the denuded wall of the red mesa. When Gid looked in the direction Will was pointing, he saw a little puff of smoke drifting away.

"Yeah, I see him," he said.

Even as they were looking, there was another puff of smoke, followed by the rifle's report, then, a fraction of a second later, another bullet striking rock near them.

"There's only one way we're going to get him out of there," Will said.

"I know," Gid answered. "We're going to have to go after him."

"One of us needs to get to the rocks over there," Will said, pointing to a collection of boulders which were located near the base of the cliff.

"One of us?"

"That's the best place to provide cover for whichever one of us is going to climb up the side of the cliff."

"You know I can't climb up that wall. I'm afraid of heights," Gid said.

"It's your choice, Little Brother. Climb up the side of the cliff...or haul your ass across the open to get to those rocks over there."

Glaring at his brother, Gid got up, took a deep breath, then ran toward the rocks in question. "Ooooooh hell," he yelled as the bullets popped and whined, kicking up dirt all around him. Finally, with a dive that covered the last five yards, Gid made it to the rocks.

Once behind the rocks, Gid turned to look back toward his brother, giving him a little wave to let him know that he was all right. Will nodded, and Gid, now in position, began firing up toward whoever had been shooting at them.

Will looked around, then saw a possible way up the side of the canyon wall. He followed it with his eyes and saw that it led all the way to the top. Except for a few gaps, it offered cover and concealment for anyone who might climb it. It was obvious that the assailant hadn't noticed it, or he wouldn't have taken the position he now occupied, for if someone successfully negotiated the climb, he would be on top of the mesa...behind the shooter.

Will began to climb. Although the route had looked passable from the ground, climbing it proved to be very difficult. He'd been at it for nearly half an hour, and it didn't seem as if he had gained so much as an inch. However, when he looked back toward the ground he could see that he was making progress, for by now he was dangerously high.

All the time he was climbing he could hear the steady exchange of gunfire between his brother and whoever it was that attacked them.

Will clung to the side of the mountain and moved only when he had a secure handhold or foothold...tiny though it might be. Sweat poured into his eyes and he grew thirsty with the effort, but still he climbed. Then he came to a complete stop. There was no place to go from here. He hadn't noticed this gap from his observation on the ground.

"Damn," he swore under his breath, looking around. "Now what?"

From his position behind the rocks, Gid saw that his brother had stopped climbing. At first, he wondered why, then he realized that Will must have run out of hand and footholds. He realized something else, as well. Though much of Will's climb had been shielded by a long, vertical spur of rock, he was no longer shielded. If whoever it was shooting at them happened to glance over and look in the right place now, he would see Will. He would not only see him...he would have a very easy and totally unrestricted shot at him. And, because Will was having to hang on with both hands and both feet, there would be absolutely nothing Will could do to defend himself.

"Big Brother, you do get yourself, in some terrible fixes," Gid said as he fired again, hoping to keep the assailant sufficiently occupied so that he wouldn't notice Will.

Will decided that his only hope was in backtracking several feet, then starting up one of the other chutes. This he did, and though the going was very difficult, he was managing to climb again. Above him was nothing but the uninviting rock-face of the cliff. Below him was a sheer drop of more than 150 feet to the rocky canyon floor.

Will continued his climb, working hard to find the handholds and tiny crevices by which he could advance. Sweat poured into his eyes and slickened the palms of his hands, but still he climbed. He reached for a small slate outcropping, but as he put his weight on it, it failed. With a sickening sensation in his stomach, he felt himself falling.

His stomach leaped into his throat as he started to fall, and, reflexively, he reached out to grab the first thing he could. It was a juniper tree. With one hand, he managed to grab the tree and stop his fall. He was slammed against the wall, feeling the rocks scrape and tear at his flesh. He flailed against the wall with his other hand until he managed to get a hold.

After catching his breath, Will began to climb again. After two minutes of climbing it began to get a little easier, then easier still, until finally he reached a ledge which showed signs of having been a trail at one time, possibly a trail which had existed until erosion took the bottom part of it away. The trail improved and widened until he could walk upright. Shortly after that, he made it to the top.

Will saw the assailant then, no more than twenty-five yards away from him, peering down toward the canyon floor, totally unaware that Will had reached the top.

"Looking for someone?" Will asked casually.

"What the hell?" the gunman gasped, spinning around. "How'd you get up here? They ain't no way a mountain goat coulda come up."

"I'm not a mountain goat," Will said. "I'm a Missouri mule."

The two men stood on top of the mesa, silhouetted against the brilliant blue sky. Because the assailant had been using his rifle, both now had their pistols holstered, and for a moment they formed an eerie tableau, a moment frozen in eternity.

"Hell, let's do it," the assailant said, his hand dipping for his gun even as he spoke.

The assailant's gun didn't even break leather before Will's gun was out and booming. Will's bullet hit him in the chest, and the assailant stood there for a moment, looking on in total surprise. He tried to take a step forward, lost his balance, then fell.

Holstering his pistol, Will moved quickly to him, then stood, looking down at him.

"Why'd you ambush us?" he asked.

"I seen that fella back in town give you some money to bring Cat back to him. And I know there ain't no way *El Jefe* is goin' to let her go, so I figured I might as well have the money for myself." He coughed, and a little trickle of blood came from his mouth.

"Who's *El Jefe?*"

"You try 'n' bring that girl back, you'll find out who *El Jefe* is," the assailant said.

"Will! Will, you all right?" Will heard Gid's voice calling anxiously.

Will raised up, then walked over to the edge to call down. "I'm all right, Gid. Round up our horses. I'll be right down."

Will walked back over to the assailant. "I'm going to have to leave you here," he said. "Anybody in town you want me to tell about you?"

Even as he was asking the question, though, he knew it would go unanswered. The would-be robber was dead.

Chapter Two

When the boys reached Afton, they boarded their horses, then went across the street to the hotel.

"The way I figure it, folks aren't likely to be all that cooperative with someone who comes in and just starts asking a lot of questions," Will said. "I think we should take our time and just look around for a while."

"You're probably right," Gid agreed. "What say we start by having a little supper?"

"All right," Will agreed.

They had supper in the nearest restaurant, then, while Gid had a second dessert, Will decided to take a walk around the town.

It was dark now, and the street was lighted only by spills of yellow from the open doors and windows of the saloons and cantinas. High overhead, the stars winked brightly, while over a distant mesa the moon hung like a large, silver wheel. He could hear music: the thrum of guitars; a lilting song in a language he couldn't understand; and from somewhere, the single, clarion sound of a trumpet.

When Will reached the end of the street, he turned and started back. That was when two men with knives jumped from the shadows between the buildings and attacked. He responded quickly, avoiding one blade, but catching the tip of the other in his side. One inch closer and he would have been disemboweled.

One of them moved in to try to finish Will off, but Will dropped to the ground, twisted and thrust his feet out, catching the attacker on his chest, driving him back several feet.

Will sent a booted foot whistling toward one of them, catching the man in the groin. Then he lunged upward and rammed a hard fist into the teeth of the other man. He felt the man's teeth loosen and crack.

Then breaking off the fight, they ran around the corner and disappeared into the shadows before Will could get a good look at them.

"Mister," a pained voice called from the shadows of a nearby building. "Help me, mister."

"Where are you?"

"Back here, on the ground."

Disregarding his own wound, Will moved into the

shadows. There he saw a man on his hands and knees, trying to rise. Will helped him to his feet.

"Much obliged," the man said. "Those two jumped me and woulda robbed me if you hadn't come along to pull 'em off me."

Will chuckled dryly. "Hate to disappoint you, mister," he said. "But I didn't pull 'em off you. They came for me, too."

"They musta thought you were comin' to my rescue," the man said. "And, whether you meant to do it or not, it all comes out the same. Could you... could you help me back to the hotel?"

"Sure, be glad to," Will said, taking the man's arm around his shoulder and walking with him for support.

"The name's Welch, John Sydney Welch," the wounded man said. "I own the Red Rock Ranch. Ever heard of it?"

"Can't say as I have," Will admitted.

"It's some west of here. I come into town from time to time for supplies, and the two Mexes must've seen me over at the general store when I was puttin' in my order. I guess they figured that if I had enough money to pay for the supplies, I would have enough money to steal."

"Do you?"

"Have enough money to steal, you mean?"

"Yes. Because if you do, and you have it on you, part of this is your own fault."

"It doesn't take much money to tempt someone like those two galoots," John Sydney replied. Will noticed that his question had gone unanswered, and he smiled. Perhaps the man wasn't as incautious as it first seemed.

"By the way," John Sydney continued, "if you're interested in work, I'd be glad to sign you on."

"Thanks," Will said. "But right now, I've got a job."

"Doin' what?"

"Looking for someone. A man has paid my brother and me to find a woman and take her back to him. The woman's name is Cat Clay. She's supposed to work in one of the saloons here. Ever heard of her?"

John Sydney shook his head. "No, I can't say as I have," he said.

"Anyway, I have to confess, I'm not cut out to be a cowhand," Will added.

"No, I don't expect you would be. At least, you don't have that kind of look about you," John Sydney said. "That makes it all the more probable that you might be just what I'm lookin' for."

"Now I am curious. You said you own a ranch. If you aren't looking for a cowhand, just what are you looking for?"

"I'm lookin' for someone who isn't afraid of a fight and who is good with guns."

"That kind of man can be dangerous," Will warned.

"It would take that kind of a man. The job I'm wantin' him to do is dangerous," John Sydney said. "Ah, here's the hotel. Again, I thank you for helpin' me."

"Glad I could be of service."

John Sydney wanted to go the last few yards on his own, so Will let him do it, though he did follow him into the lobby.

"Father!" a woman's voice called, and Will looked up to see a beautiful young woman standing halfway down the stairs. She was tall and slender with blonde hair and blue eyes. She hurried across the lobby to her father. "What happened? Are you all right?"

"I'm fine," John Sydney said. "Thanks to this gentleman," he added, pointing to Will. "Two *hombres* jumped me, intent on cuttin' my throat and robbin' me, I suppose. But this fella came along and ran them off. Mister...uh, you know, I don't believe I caught your name."

"Crockett. Will Crockett."

"Mister Crockett, this is my daughter."

"I'm very obliged to you for saving my father, Mister Crockett."

Will smiled. "Well, Miss Welch, much as I would like for you to think I'm a hero, I have to confess that I was drawn into the fracas. I was just walking around, polite as you please. They jumped me before I even saw them."

"And yet you beat them off? That's all the more

reason to...oh...you're hurt!"

Will didn't realize it, but by now he made quite a sight. He was holding his hand over his wound, but the blood was seeping around his fingers. That had been going on for several minutes and, by now, his cotton shirt and denim trousers were soaked with blood.

"Where are you staying? Do you have a room?" Caroline asked.

"Yes, ma'am," Will said. He waved his hand and the blood shined red in the soft light of the hotel lobby. "I have one right here in the hotel."

"Go up to your room, quickly," Caroline said. "What number is it? I'll get some things to take care of your wound."

"It's number twelve," Will said. "And I think it might be a good idea if I did lie down at that."

As Will started up the stairs, he discovered that the wound was bothering him more than he'd first thought. He had to stop halfway up and lean against the wall to get his breath. When he went on, he left a stain of blood on the wall.

Once inside his room, he ripped the bedsheet in two and wrapped it around his side, pressing it tightly against his wound. When the crude bandage was in place, he lay on the bed, closed his eyes, and fell asleep.

Will opened his eyes. Something had awakened him

and he lay very still. The doorknob turned, and Will was up, reaching for the gun that lay on the table by his bed.

He moved as quickly as a cat, forgetting the wound in his stomach. But the wound didn't let him forget, and he sucked in a gasp of air through clenched teeth as a bolt of pain shot through him.

Moving despite the pain, Will stepped to the side of the door, while at the same time cocking his pistol. Naked from the waist up, he felt the night air on his skin. His senses were alert, his body alive with readiness.

Will could hear someone breathing on the other side of the door. A thin shaft of hall light shot underneath. From somewhere in the night, a guitar played and someone laughed. He got a whiff of the scent of lilacs then, the same scent he had noticed earlier, and he smiled as he remembered the girl's promise to bring material for treating his wound.

"Miss Welch?" he called.

"Yes. I wasn't sure you would be awake," Caroline called back.

Will eased the hammer down on the pistol, then opened the door to let a wide bar of light spill into the room. The hall lantern was backlighting the thin cotton dress the girl was wearing, and he could see her body in shadow, beneath the cloth.

"Come on in," Will invited, stepping back to let her

inside. He lit the candle on his table and a golden bubble of light illuminated the room.

She held up some bandages and a jar of salve. "I just took care of my father and he's resting. If you would like I can dress your wound as well."

"All right," Will agreed. He carefully unwound the bandage he had made from the bedsheet, then lay back on his bed and loosened his belt. He slid his trousers down a few inches, exposing the entire length of the wound.

"How does it look?" Will asked.

She looked down at his wound, at his flat stomach, then, gently, she reached out and touched him. Her fingers felt cool.

"I'd better clean it," she said. She walked over to the chifforobe where a basin and a pitcher of water stood. Pouring water into the basin, she brought it back to the bed and with the soap she had brought with her, began gently bathing his stomach. Within a few minutes she had washed away all the dried blood and was now looking at the cut. It was thin and clean.

"What do you think?" Will asked.

She put her hand back on his stomach. "The wound itself doesn't look that bad. It's not that deep and the bleeding has stopped. Now that it's clean, a little of this salve is all it needs."

"What's your name?" Will asked as she applied the salve.

21

"You know my name. It's Miss Welch."

Will chuckled, then reached up to lay his hand on hers. "Don't you think that, under the circumstances, I mean me half-naked and you, with your hands on my body, that I should know your first name?"

She smiled at him. "My name is Caroline, and I think you may be presuming too much."

"Could be," Will agreed.

Outside, in the darkness of the town, Will heard a rider pass, his horse's hoofbeats ringing hollowly on the quiet street. From a nearby saloon he heard a man's low, rumbling voice, followed by the laughter of several patrons, a woman's high-pitched trill being the most discernible. On the prairie he heard a coyote howl.

Caroline had been sitting on the side of the bed while applying the salve, and now she got up and walked over to the window, pulled the curtain to one side and looked out.

"What are you looking for out there?'" Will asked.

"I'm looking for all my tomorrows," she answered. She turned away from the window. "Don't you ever look for your tomorrows, Mister Crockett?"

"It's Will, and no I never do."

"Why not, Mister Will Crockett?"

"Because I don't have any tomorrows," Will said easily.

Chapter Three

Twenty miles southwest of Afton was a small settlement called Carmen. Carmen was significant only because it was the first settlement on the American side of the border. It existed to serve the ranching community nearby. At one time there had been many ranches, but now there were only three.

One was John Sydney Welch's ranch, called the Red Rock. John Sydney's ranch was a normal-sized ranch, old and established. It had fit in well with all the neighboring ranches, that is, when there had been neighboring ranches.

The second ranch was a newer, spreading conglomerate called High Point. High Point was owned by a man everyone called "The Boss", or more specifically *"El Jefe"*, and it had been cobbled together of smaller ranches whose owners had sold out to him. Its acreage had also been swollen by the Boss's illegal, though unchallenged, practice of filing homestead claims under fictitious names on several tracts, then "selling" them to himself.

The result was that High Point was now nearly as large, in terms of acreage, as the nearby ranch of Tularosa, a vast estate, unchanged since it was given to the family of Don Jose Luis de la Fernandez by a Spanish Land Grant. Of course, Tularosa, being old and established, was a much better piece of property. It could boast proven wells, large, comfortable houses, sturdy barns, stables, and an extensive network of line shacks.

El Jefe had made a few attempts to buy Tularosa, but Fernandez had turned him down. The result was an intense enmity between *El Jefe* and Fernandez. John Sydney Welch, and his Red Rock Ranch, was caught in the middle.

When Fernandez was born, Rancho Tularosa was in Mexico, thus, Jose Luis de la Fernandez was a Mexican citizen. But he was also a citizen of the United States by virtue of the fact that all of New Mexico had, since his birth, been ceded to the United States. Although they were now American citizens, the Fernandez family still followed Spanish customs of the old ways. Because of that, Jose Luis's younger brother, Alfredo, traveled from his home in Buenaventura to visit Jose Luis and secure his brother's blessings on his upcoming marriage. Alfredo brought several of his servants, his bride-to-be, nineteen-year-old Violetta Martinez, and her servants with him.

In most of the towns along the border, the Americans and the Mexicans got along well, but in Carmen, the enmity that existed between High Point and Tularosa spilled over into the town as well.

Carmen was a village of two dozen adobe buildings, scattered around a dusty plaza, baking under the hot New Mexico sun. Fully one quarter of the buildings in town were drinking establishments, called cantinas by the Mexicans, and saloons by the Americans.

High Point riders, most of whom had come over from the ranches that had been bought out by *El Jefe*, frequented a place called the Americana Saloon when they were in town. Although the outside of the Americana looked like every other building in Carmen, inside, the owner made every effort to try to make it look as "un-Mexican" as he could. The focal point of everyone who entered the Americana Saloon was the large painting of George Washington, which hung behind the bar. The saloon served only beer and bourbon. A sign on the wall read:

ANYONE WHO ORDERS TEQUILA WILL BE PUT OUT OF THIS ESTABLISHMENT.

The Americana Saloon was the only place in town that had a piano, and it was grinding away as a handful of

High Point men sat around a table, talking.

"They say this Alfredo Fernandez is real good with a gun. Makes a body wonder what he's really comin' up here for."

"It's just like they's a sayin' it is. He's comin' here to get his brother's say-so so he can marry that little ole girl."

"Don't seem to me like a full-grow'd man ought to have to ask his brother's permission just so as he can get married."

"Yeah, well, that's the way it is with them Mexicans."

"Wonder what the girl looks like?"

"She's a real good-looker. I seen her an' her family last Sunday mornin' when they come into town to go to church."

"Damn, Buster! You was in church?"

Everyone laughed.

"No," Buster answered. "I was just headin' back to the ranch from a night of drinkin'."

Again, everyone laughed.

Rancho Tularosa

Don Jose Luis de la Fernandez was fifty-four years old. His brother, Alfredo, was forty-three. Jose Luis had married late in life but was now enjoying the fruits of a family. He had a beautiful wife and four children, ranging in ages from five to thirteen years. Alfredo had never been married before but was about to take a bride who was many years younger than he. That was not unusual in the Fernandez family. Family tradition was not the only reason Alfredo was visiting Tularosa. Alfredo knew that his brother would need help if the war that everyone was talking about really did begin. Alfredo, who lived on family holdings south of the border, was a provisional colonel in the Mexican Federal Reserve. He had recently been involved in a confrontation with the Sonora Bandidos. During the encounter, he'd fought with such honor that he was awarded a medal by the Mexican government.

Jose Luis and Alfredo had just ridden to the top of a rocky mesa. From this vantage point they could see thousands of acres of Tularosa. Most of the land was dry, baked brown under the relentless summer sun, but a long thin line of green snaked its way across the valley floor. The green was the vegetation that grew alongside the river, where the cattle congregated both for water and food. Because of the scarcity of grass and water in this part of the country, it required three times as many acres to support cattle here as back in Texas. That was why the ranches had to be so large.

"So, my brother, it has been a long time since you were here at Tularosa. What do you think of it now?"

"I think it is *magnifico,*" Alfredo said enthusiastically. "I think it may be the...uhn!" Alfredo suddenly put his hand to his chest. When he pulled it away, it was smeared with blood. "Jose Luis?" he asked in a pained, questioning voice.

Neither man had heard the first shot, and thus the rifle bullet that buried itself deep in Alfredo's chest was a surprise. Jose Luis heard the second shot, not only the report of the rifle, but the little thudding sound it made when it too hit Alfredo. Alfredo reeled for a second, then tumbled out of his saddle. Jose Luis pulled out his own rifle, then leaped from his saddle and knelt beside his brother.

"Alfredo!" Jose Luis shouted. He put his hand on his brother's shoulder and shook him, but he got no response. Then, sadly, he reached up to close Alfredo's eyes. His brother was dead.

As great as Jose Luis's sorrow over his brother's death, even greater was his anger and thirst for revenge. He ran to the back of the mesa and saw someone riding off in the direction of High Point. Whoever it was was well out of rifle range, but in frustration Jose Luis raised his rifle and fired at him anyway.

High Point Ranch

There were three cowboys inside the small adobe line shack. One was asleep on the bunk; the other two were sitting across a barrelhead from each other, playing cards. They were playing for matches only, but that didn't lessen the intensity of their game. When one of them took the pot with a pair of aces, the other one complained.

"You son of a bitch! Where'd you get that ace?" His oath, however, was softened by a burst of laughter.

"Don't you know? I took it from Buster's boot while he was asleep."

"Does Buster keep an ace in his boot?"

"You think he don't? I never know'd him to do anythin' honest when he could cheat."

"That's the truth. But Scarborough's just as bad."

"So's Stubby."

The cards were raked in, the deck shuffled, then dealt again.

"Who you think shot that Mexican?" the dealer asked.

"More'n likely it was Quinn Turner."

"You ask me, it was awful dumb of him. Them Mexicans over on Tularosa ain't goin' to just let that slide by like it didn't nothin' happen."

"What's got me is why *El Jefe* ain't done nothin' to Turner."

"Hell, I know why. It's 'cause *El Jefe* wants a range war with Fernandez. Wouldn't surprise me none, but what the boss put Turner up to it."

"Why would anyone actually want a range war?"

"'Cause he figures when it's all over, he'll wind up ownin' Tularosa."

"You're just talkin'."

"No, I ain't just talkin' neither. Last week one of Fernandez's riders brought back four of our cows that had strayed over onto their land. I thought it was real neighborly, but *El Jefe* said I shoulda shot 'im. He said havin' the cows with him was all the proof we needed that they'd been stole."

The cowboy on the bunk spoke for the first time.

"Seems to me like you boys should know by now to keep your mouths shut. Whatever *El Jefe's* doin' don't got nothin' to do with us. And, iffen I was you, I wouldn't go accusin' Turner neither. Leastwise, not to his face."

"You think I'm scared of Turner?"

"If you got 'ny sense you are. Turner's got that gun with 'im all the time. He even has it with 'im when he goes to take a shit."

The others laughed.

At that moment, four riders, wearing sombreros and serapes, stopped on a little hill overlooking the High Point line shack, then ground-tied their mounts about thirty yards behind them. They moved to the edge of the hill at a crouch, then looked down toward the little building.

The leader gave the signal, and all four men raised their rifles.

"Shoot!" the leader said, squeezing the trigger that sent out the first bullet.

The dealer died instantly, a bullet coming through the window to crash into the back of his head. His partner went next, a bullet in his chest. Buster, who was on the bunk, rolled onto the floor.

"Bruno!" he said. "It's the Mexicans!"

"Buster!" the wounded man on the floor called. "Buster, This is it!"

Buster crawled over to the wounded man, then saw the blood on his chest. The wound was sucking air, and Buster knew it would be over shortly. He put his hand on the wounded man's forehead, and that gesture of comfort was Buster's last mortal act, for the next bullet hit him right between the eyes. Less than a moment later, all three were dead.

"You did what?" Fernandez asked in horror.

"We have taken revenge for the murder of *om patron.*"

Fernandez pinched the bridge of his nose and was silent for a long time.

"It was not your place to do so," he said, speaking to the men who had been in Alfredo's employ and had come to New Mexico for the happy event of a wedding, only to see their *patron* murdered.

"I know he was your brother, and perhaps you would have preferred to do it yourself. But, senor, he was our *caudillo* and *venganza* was our right and our duty."

"Venganza es de Dios," Fernandez said. "It is for God, not for man." He sighed.

"I'm sorry if our action has displeased you, Senor Fernandez."

"You killed three men," Fernandez said. "If I could be sure that one of the three you killed was the one who murdered my brother, I would gladly suffer any consequences from your action. But we do not know that. They may well have been innocent men."

One of the vaqueros spit derisively. "There *are* no innocent gringos," he insisted.

Still bowing his head, almost as if he were in prayer, Fernandez dismissed the four vaqueros who had taken matters into their own hands.

"Go," Fernandez said. "Return to Mexico. *Vaya con Dios."*

"Vaya con Dios," the leader of the group said. They got on their horses then rode away. If it had been in their thoughts to depart as heroes, the folly of that idea was vividly demonstrated now as the working men and women of the ranch stood by in frightened silence.

"Jose Luis, will there be much trouble now?" Josefina, Jose Luis's wife, asked.

"I do not know," Jose Luis admitted. "Perhaps, if there are no more acts of vengeance, it will stop here. But we must, at all times, be on guard."

Chapter Four

Afton

A gentle breeze filtered through the stable. It carried
with it the aromas of a new day; frying bacon and brewing coffee from the scores of breakfasts that were being
cooked, and the strong, though not unpleasant, smell of
horseflesh and fresh hay.

After Gid and Will separated the night before, Gid
had finished his dessert, then made the rounds of the
saloons in town. He didn't see Will again, but it didn't
concern him. He knew that Will was a big boy and could
take care of himself. It was after midnight when Gid
climbed the stairs of the hotel. But when he opened
the door to the room and saw that Will had a woman
with him, and not knowing that his brother had been
wounded, he thought that it might be best if he spent the
night somewhere else. He quietly withdrew and spent

the night in the stable with their horses.

After rubbing his eyes, Gid stretched, then walked up to the open door of the stable and stared out onto the street. The town appeared as quiet this morning as it had been boisterous the night before. Merchants were already preparing for the day's commerce, and the baskets of potatoes, onions, and peaches, that were displayed on the porches in front of the stores shared space with ax handles, grub hoes, and brooms. A few doors down the street the butcher was dressing a side of beef while a dozen dogs waited expectantly for the scraps he was throwing them. A freight wagon lumbered slowly through the town.

Gid walked across the street, picking his way through the piles of pungent horse apples, until he reached the restaurant that was next door to the hotel.

The restaurant was a long, narrow building, with a line of tables running along the right wall, and a counter stretching down the left side. Gid walked to the last table, then sat down. An old Mexican woman came to take his order.

"Si, senor?"

"You have American food, don't you?" Gid asked. "Bacon? Eggs? Flapjacks?"

"Si, senor."

"Well, I don't want any breakfast yet, I'm waiting

for my brother."

The woman turned and started back.

"Wait!" Gid called.

She stopped.

"I will have some coffee while I'm waiting, though. And maybe half a dozen flapjacks, and a few strips of bacon. That ought to hold me over till he gets here. Then I'll have breakfast."

Gid was just finishing his "appetizers" when Will arrived.

"Boy, am I glad to see you," Gid said, washing down the last bite of pancake with coffee. "I don't know how much longer I would have been able to wait. I was about to go ahead and order breakfast." He held up his hand to get the waitress's attention. "Those two breakfasts I said I would be wanting? You can bring 'em now."

"Si, senor."

Will took his seat. "First bed I've slept in for a while... it was sort of hard to get out of it this morning."

"Yeah, especially since you probably didn't sleep that much," Gid suggested.

"What do you mean?"

"I saw the woman. Why do you think I spent the night in the stable?"

"You saw the woman? On, you mean Caroline?"

"I didn't hang around long enough to ask her her

name."

"It's not what you think, Little Brother."

Gid chuckled. "Whatever you say."

The old woman set two steaming plates down in front of the boys.

"Any luck last night?" Will asked as he began putting butter on his biscuit. "Did you find out anything about this Cat Clay woman we came here to find?"

"No. Fact is, when I finally got around to asking about her, I couldn't find anyone who had ever even heard of her."

Gid saw the front door to the restaurant open and a man came inside, then stood there for a moment. When he noticed the back table, he started toward it.

"Someone's coming," Gid said.

When Will turned toward the door, he saw John Sydney Welch.

"Good mornin', Mister Crockett," John Sydney greeted. "I hope you will let me repay your kindness to me last night by buyin' your breakfast. And your friend's breakfast as well."

"This is my brother, Gid," Will said. "And I'd better warn you before you get too generous that this isn't his first."

"That's quite all right. After what you did for me last night, it's little enough in repayment."

"Just what did you do for this fella?" Gid asked.

"A couple of Mexicans jumped him," Will explained. "When I came by, they left him and jumped me instead. I fought them off and picked up a little scratch to show for it."

"Did my daughter come by to tend to your wound?" John Sydney asked. "She's a good nurse, but unfortunately, she gets a lot of practice."

"Yes, she did stop by. She cleaned me up and put that horse salve on me and I think I'm as good as new," Will said.

Gid looked at Will with a silent question, and an almost imperceptible squinting of the eyes answered it.

"So that's..." Gid started to say about the woman he saw in Will's room, but when Will affirmed it by nodding, Gid didn't finish his sentence.

"Oh, Mister Crockett, don't think the salve Caroline used was horse salve. It is the finest medicinal herb in the Southwest. Made by Indians, you know," John Sydney said. "Do you mind if I join you gentlemen?"

"No, go ahead."

John Sydney sat down and when the old woman came over, he ordered bacon and eggs.

"I've got a proposition for you, Mister Crockett. Actually, for both of you if you would consider it."

"This would have to do with what you mentioned last night? You need to hire someone who is good with guns for a dangerous job, I believe you said."

"Yes," John Sydney answered. "The pay will be good. Very good."

"How good?"

"I'll give you five hundred dollars apiece."

Gid whistled. "That *is* good," he said. "That's more'n we're getting to look for the girl that no one seems to have heard of."

"Doesn't matter," Will replied. "We agreed to find the girl and take her back, and that's what we're going to do."

"I admire your principles," John Sydney said. "All the more reason why I'd like to have you workin' with me." He took a piece of paper from his pocket. "Look, I'm goin' to write my name and directions on how to get to the Red Rock Ranch," he said. He put the pencil between his teeth and twisted around a few times, making more of the lead available. Then, smoothing the paper, he started to write. Before he formed the first letter, though, he looked up. "Can you boys read?"

Will nodded. "We can read."

"Good. Once you find the girl you are lookin' for and you're finished with your job, you come on out to the Red Rock Ranch. The job will still be waitin' for you...unless *El Jefe* has already won the battle by then."

Will looked up with a start. "What's that?" he asked.

"I said the job will still be waitin' for you."

"No, the other thing. Something about *El Jefe?*"

"Not *any El Jefe, the El Jefe*. The Boss Man is what that means, but I've never heard him called anything but *El Jefe*. I don't even think I even know his real name."

"What is it, Will? Why are you so interested in this *El Jefe?*" Gid asked.

"The man who ambushed us back in the canyon mentioned him," Will said. "He said that there was no way *'El Jefe'* would let the girl go. That's what he called him. *El Jefe*. The Boss Man."

"What kind of battle are you and *El Jefe* in?" Will asked.

"Right now, we are in no battle at all," John Sydney replied. "*El Jefe* and a Mexican fella named Jose Luis de la Fernandez are the only ones who are actually fightin' a battle. They're the two biggest ranches in the area, and when this is all over...there's only goin' to be one left. I'm afraid that whoever is left will come after me."

"If that happens, do you think you and your hands could hold 'em off? Even with the addition of a couple of guns?" Will asked.

"I don't know," John Sydney admitted. "I only know I'm not goin' to roll over and play dead for either one of 'em."

"This here Boss Man fella, or *El Jefe* or whatever in hell you call him," Gid asked, "do you know if he has a woman with him? A woman named Cat Clay?"

"If I thought it would get you to come with me, I'd tell you he did," John Sydney replied. "But the truth is, I don't know if he has a woman with him or not."

"When are you going back to your ranch?" Will asked.

"Soon as my wagon is loaded," John Sydney replied.

"I'll tell you what. Let me look around town a bit. It could be that we'll talk again before you leave," Will suggested.

"I'll be in town for as long as you see my wagon over there in front of the general store," John Sydney said. "Right now, I'm figurin' on pullin' out about mid-afternoon. That'll put me back to Red Rock o'bout nightfall."

When Gid and Will stepped into the saloon, it was nearly empty, though there was someone sitting down at the far end of the bar, very carefully nursing a drink. The bartender was washing glasses, and someone was sweeping the floor. At a table in the back of the room, a large man sat playing solitaire.

"What'll it be, gents?" the bartender asked.

"Beer," Will ordered. With a nod, the bartender drew two mugs, then set them on the bar. "And give my friend at the end of the bar whatever he's drinking," Will added.

"Your friend?" the bartender said with a snort. "Hell, that's the town drunk, mister."

"You're not telling me who I can have as a friend, are you?" Will asked.

"No, sir, not me," the bartender said. "I was just pointin'

out that he's the town drunk, that's all."

"Give him a drink."

The bartender nodded, then took a bottle down to the end of the bar.

The drunk, seeing that he was about to get a refill, finished his drink quickly, then held the glass out. The bartender filled it.

"Give me the bottle," Will said and, taking the bottle, he moved down to the end of the bar to talk to the drunk. Will had been around the smell of unwashed bodies, putrefying wounds, and battlefield death, but the stench of this man was almost unbearable. Nevertheless, he got close enough to pour another drink into the glass which the drunk happily held out to him.

"You come in here a lot, do you?" Will asked.

"Every day," the drunk answered. "I come into here, then I go to Mister Cannon's establishment...that's the saloon just down the street, then I go into the other two. But this one is the best."

"Do you know any of the women?"

The smile left the drunk's face. "Mister, I'm an alcoholic...I'm not stupid. You see the wretch that I have become. Do you think any woman...even a lady of the evening... would have anything to do with me?"

"I mean, do you know any of them by name? I'm looking for one woman in particular."

"I know some of the names," the drunk replied. He held out his empty glass, and, once more, Will filled it. The drunk tossed the drink down as if it were water. "Who are you looking for?" he asked.

"I'm looking for a woman named Cat Clay."

Will saw recognition register in the drunk's eyes, but then he said nothing.

"I want to pay you for the drinks," he said.

"Good, good, that's the whole point. You can pay me by giving me the information I'm looking for. Do you know Cat Clay?"

Without answering, the drunk got up and walked away. At first, Will thought he was going to leave, but, to his surprise, the drunk walked over to the piano and sat down.

The drunk looked at the keyboard for a minute, then he put his hands out and began to play. Will expected some bouncy tune, such as *Buffalo Gals*. Instead, to his total surprise, the beautiful notes of a classical piece of music filled the room. The music spilled out, a steady, never-wavering string of melodic phrases with a single melody weaving through the piece like a thread of gold woven through the finest cloth. Suddenly, and unexpectedly, Will experienced a moment of deja vu. Then he realized that he had heard this same piece of music before. *Mozart's Sonata in F Major.*

Will's mother had loved music, and once, just before the war, a concert pianist had visited Kansas City. Will took her, and Katie Ann McMurtry, the young woman who lived on the adjacent farm, to hear him. Katie Ann loved music as much as Will and his mother did. Will's father hadn't gone because, in his words, "Listening to that kind of music makes beads of sweat as big as the end of my thumb pop out on me." And Gid evidently got his musical appreciation from his father, because there was no way Will could make Gid go with them. So, it had been just Will, his mother, and Katie Ann. Now, as he listened to this man play the piano, he let time and distance slide away. There had not been a war, there was no Quantrill, and Lawrence, Kansas, had never happened. Will and his brother were not unsettled men roaming the West, unwilling and unable to return home to Missouri. He could almost believe that he could leave this place and ride back to the farm, to see the house and barn and outbuildings standing, to see his father working the field, and his mother baking in the kitchen. All those memories and all that emotion were triggered by the music the town drunk was playing.

But they were memories only, for the white house and the red barn of their Missouri farm no longer existed. They had been burned to the ground, and today not even a pile of blackened ash marked the spot where the buildings once stood. The only thing to give any indication of what had once been there were the two graves in which the charred remains of Will and Gid's mother and father lay. They had been killed, and their farm burned, by Jayhawkers.

It was that incident that brought Will and Gid into the war, fighting as Bushwhackers in Quantrill's guerrilla band. It was that experience too that had set the boys on the trail, for the amnesty that was promised—and delivered to the other soldiers of the South—was denied the men who had fought with Quantrill.

Will looked back toward the bar, at his brother. He was looking into his beer. The music had meant nothing to Gid, so he was totally oblivious to the emotional storm Will was experiencing at the moment.

When the song was over, the man got up and walked out of the saloon without saying another word.

Chapter Five

"Where is she? Is she here?" a woman asked.

Will had been looking toward the door through which the drunk had just exited when he heard the question. Looking around, he saw a woman standing at the foot of the stairs.

"Where is who?" Will asked.

"Cat Clay. Is she down here?"

"What makes you think she might be?"

"I heard Mister Hilbronner playing the song he always plays for her, so I thought, maybe, Cat had come back."

"She's not here, but I'm looking for her if you know where she is," Will said. "By the way, what's your name?"

"My name is Dinah Perkins and I..." The woman stopped in mid-sentence then and looked around the room nervously. "First, I want to know who you are. Did *El Jefe* send you?"

"And I want to know who is *El Jefe*, Dinah?" Will asked. "And where is Cat? Is she with *El Jefe*?"

"No, who are you?" Dinah asked again, more nervous than before.

"I'm a friend," Will said. "I'm a friend of Cat's, and I'm looking for her."

Dinah shook her head no. "I don't believe you. I've never seen you before, and I know Cat's friends."

"I'm a friend from her past."

Dinah's eyes grew flat and distant. "Cat has no past," she said. "None of us do. We have no past, and we have no future. If you were really a friend of Cat's, you would know that." She turned and started back up the stairs.

"Wait, I just want to—"

From behind him, Will heard the sound of a chair scooting across the floor, then he felt the floor jar as something big and heavy moved toward him.

"Mister, I think it's about time you left," a man's voice said. When Will looked around he could almost believe that a tree had suddenly grown up beside him. The big man who had been sitting at the back of the room, playing solitaire, had given up his game to come over and confront Will directly. The man was at least six feet eight inches tall, with a bald head that looked like a cannonball. He had no neck, wide shoulders, and massive arms which hung, gorilla-like, by his sides.

"I've got a better idea," Will said. "You leave!" Moving quickly, Will picked up a chair, then brought it down, hard, on the giant's head. The giant just smiled at him. Will was unable to believe that the giant was still on his feet.

The giant swung one massive hand at Will. Will managed to throw up his hands and turn aside to protect himself. Even so, the glancing blow sent tingling sensations through his entire body, down his arms and into his hands. He had the distinct feeling that, even if he had wanted to use his gun against this man now, he would be unable to do so. He didn't think he could even hold a pistol, let alone pull it from his holster.

"Will! Get the hell away from him!" Gid shouted.

Heeding his brother's advice, Will backed away. Still smiling, the giant started after Will, but Gid stepped in between them and sent a hard, smashing blow to the giant's jaw. Gid was a very strong man, and Will had seen him in fights before. Ordinarily, Will knew, this punch would bring a man down. The only effect the giant showed, however, was to stop grinning.

A customer came in off the street at the precise moment Gid hit the giant. "Hey!" he called back over his shoulder. "The giant and that big fella are goin' at it!"

Within seconds there were half a dozen new customers in the bar. Also, the woman who had started upstairs after Will's questioning, stopped and came back down. A moment later she was joined by three or four more women, in various stages of undress. They, like the men in the front of the saloon, stood by in fascination, as the fight between Gid and the giant continued.

The giant swung a large, clublike blow, which Gid was able to avoid. Gid came up on his feet and began dancing around, while the giant stood flat-footed, watching Gid dance and weave, waiting for his opportunity. The giant swung again, as wildly as before, and Gid countered with a swift left jab that caught the giant square in the face. Despite the power of the blow, the giant just laughed it off.

Surprisingly, Will was able to observe the fight with an almost detached interest, curious as to how Gid would handle him. He knew that Gid combined strength with quickness and agility, but he also knew that Gid had never gone up against anyone as big or as powerful as this man.

After evading another of the big man's swings, Gid counterpunched with a second quick jab. Again, the giant just laughed it off. As the fight progressed, it became apparent that Gid could hit the giant, almost at will, but since he was bobbing and weaving, he couldn't set himself for a telling blow, and so his scores didn't faze the giant at all.

Gid hit the big man in the stomach several times, obviously hoping to find a soft spot, but none was there.

Giving that up, he started throwing punches at the giant's head, but they were just as ineffectual until a quick opening allowed him to slam a left, square into the giant's face. Will saw the giant's already-flat nose go even flatter under Gid's fist. From that, Will knew that it had been broken. The nose started bleeding profusely, and the blood ran across the big man's teeth. It was a gruesome sight, especially as the giant continued to grin wickedly, seemingly unperturbed by his injury.

Gid kept trying to hit the nose again, but the giant started protecting it, which indicated to Will that the nose was undoubtedly hurting. The giant, nonetheless, continued to throw great swinging blows toward Gid, who managed to slip by any real impact, catching them on his forearms and shoulders. Will feared that if just one of them connected with his brother's head, Gid would be finished.

A moment later, Gid managed to get another sharp, bruising jab through to the giant's nose, and for the first time, the giant let out a bellow of pain. But it was clear that the triumph would be momentary, for the thunderous punches that had repeatedly assailed Gid's shoulders and forearms were beginning to tell as he moved more slowly. Then the giant managed to land a straight, short right, and Gid fell to his hands and knees.

"Gid!" Will shouted.

With a yell of victory, the giant rushed over to him and tried to kick him, but at the last second, Gid rolled to one side. He hopped up again before the giant could recover for a second kick and, while the big man was still off balance, sent a brutal punch straight into the giant's groin.

When the giant instinctively dropped both hands to his groin, Gid slugged him in the Adam's apple. The giant clutched his neck with both hands and sagged, gagging, to his knees. Gid hit him one final time, putting everything he had into a blow to the point of the chin. The giant fell facedown, unconscious.

The onlookers were at first stunned, then they all started talking at once.

"Did you kill him?" someone asked.

"No, I don't think so," Gid replied, his breathing coming now in ragged gasps.

"Well, if you didn't kill him, I think it would be best not to be around when the big son of a bitch wakes up."

"Yeah, I think you're right," Gid said, going over to retrieve his hat. "That sounds like a good idea to me. Come on, Big Brother, let's get out of here."

"Wait!" someone called from the stairway. It was Dinah, the woman Will had been talking to earlier, and he went over to see what she wanted.

"*El Jefe* took Cat with him," she said. "I don't think

she really wanted to go, but he sort of forced her if you know what I mean."

"You mean he tied her up and took her as his prisoner?"

"No, nothing like that."

"Then, no, I don't know what you mean. How could he 'force' her to go with him?"

"He is a very, uh, persuasive man," Dinah said.

"Where did she go, do you know?"

"I think he took her to Carmen."

"Carmen?"

"It's a little town south and west of here. On the Mexican border."

"Thanks," Will said.

"But I'm telling you now, it won't do you any good if you do find her," the woman said. "She won't go with you."

"Why don't we let her decide that?" Will suggested.

The woman shook her head. "It won't be up to her."

"What do you mean, it won't be up to her?"

"That's what I've been trying to tell you. Whether or not she leaves Carmen depends on *El Jefe*."

"What does he have to do with it?"

"Some people think there are no slaves anymore. But that isn't true. Cat is a slave, as surely as anyone ever was. She is a slave, and *El Jefe* is her master. He owns her," Dinah said in a matter-of-fact voice.

Rancho Tularosa

Although Jose Luis had doubled the guard for the last two nights, the anticipated attack from High Point never occurred. Jose Luis was certain that the bodies had been discovered by now. Why had there been no retaliation?

High Point

Jose Luis was correct in assuming that the bodies had been discovered. *El Jefe* had not only found them, he had already buried them. Where Jose Luis made his mistake was in assuming that *El Jefe* would have enough concern for his cowboys to want to conduct a retaliatory attack.

"Let me take some of the boys, Boss," one of the cowboys who had been a particularly close friend of Buster's said. "They killed three of ours, we'll kill three of theirs."

"No," El Jefe said, holding up his hand. "We have no proof that Fernandez was behind this. I think it's just best to wait, and not make any move until we are sure of what we are doing."

"All I can say, Boss Man, is you got a cooler head than I do."

That was true. The cowboy was reacting on raw emotion. His friends had been killed, and he was hurt, and wanted to hurt back. *El Jefe* wasn't hurt. He felt no emotion whatsoever, no sense of loss over his men, no burning need to pay anyone back for their deaths. Their deaths meant nothing to him, but tactical advantage meant everything.

He would make his move against Fernandez someday, but only when the time was absolutely right, and only when there would be a definite financial advantage for him.

Rancho Tularosa

"If you have no objections, senorita," Jose Luis said, "I will bury my brother here, at Rancho Tularosa. It is where I wish to be buried and where my family will be buried. He will be with his loved ones."

"Senor, it is not my place to say where he should be buried," Violetta Martinez replied, surprised that she had been consulted.

"But it is. In another day you would have been his widow, and the decision of his final resting place would have been yours."

"Then I say, let us bury him here," Violetta said. "I am sure he will rest in peace, knowing that he has the love of his brother and his brother's family to watch over him."

"Thank you, Violetta, you are most gracious," Jose Luis said. He nodded to his foreman, who left quietly to prepare the grave at the family cemetery, where Jose Luis and Alfredo Fernandez's parents, one of Jose Luis's children, and the father and mother of Jose Luis's wife already lay buried.

Although it was a small funeral, it was conducted with great dignity, and in addition to everyone from the ranch, nearly all the Mexicans and a dozen or so Americans came out from Carmen. Padre Avendano, of the local mission, conducted the service.

When Violetta Martinez, still dressed in funeral black, returned from the burial of her fiancé, she went into the small family chapel just off the main living room and lit a candle. Then she knelt in front of the altar and prayed very hard, not only for Alfredo's soul but for her own, because she believed that his getting killed was her fault.

Her marriage had been arranged by Violetta's father. Her father knew that such a marriage was a wonderful match because Don Alfredo de la Fernandez was not only a member of the wealthy Fernandez family, he was also the owner of a large ranch in northern Mexico. He was also a well-known hero who had fought and defeated the Sonora Bandidos.

But Alfredo was forty-three years old and Violetta was only nineteen. If she married someone that old, she would become an old woman before her time. During the long journey up to Rancho Tularosa, she had prayed, unceasingly, for something to happen that would prevent the marriage.

Now there would be no wedding because Alfredo was dead, and Violetta was certain she was the cause of it. Her prayers had been answered but in such a cruel way.

By the time Violetta got up from her knees, she knew what she must do. She would stay with Jose Luis and his family and be the sister to them that she would have been had she married Alfredo. And she would never marry, but remain true to Alfredo's memory for as long as she lived. It was a penance she owed for the sin she had committed.

"But, of course, we would be happy to have you stay with us," Josefina said when Violetta told her of her plans. "Jose Luis, do you see how sweet she is?"

"Yes," Jose Luis agreed. He kept to himself any worry about the range war he knew was about to erupt. In fact, he had thought of sending Josefina, their children, and Violetta back to Mexico. The only reason he did not was because he was afraid that they would be subjected to a greater danger during the trip back.

"I have an idea," Josefina suggested. "We can send Violetta and the children to the school in Carmen. Miss Welch is a wonderful teacher, and Violetta can learn much from her."

"Yes," Jose Luis agreed. "That is a good idea." Miss Welch, he knew, was the daughter of the owner of the Red Rock Ranch. Even though he was an American, John Sydney Welch had long been a good neighbor. He was neutral in the disagreement between Rancho Tularosa and High Point Ranch. Because of that, Jose Luis believed that anyone in his care—or in the care of John Sydney Welch's daughter—would be safe in a range war, no matter how ferocious the fighting might become.

Violetta was equally happy about the decision. She very much wanted to finish her education, and by helping to watch over the Fernandez children, she believed she would be paying the debt of honor she owed the Fernandez family.

Chapter Six

Berto Bolanos raised the binoculars to his eyes and looked
down toward the little camp. There were two wagons and
four men in the camp. Berto was certain there would be
something valuable inside the wagons.

Berto had bandoliers of rifle ammunition that crisscrossed his chest, a pistol belt full of cartridges around
his waist, and a long knife in a scabbard that hung down
his back, just behind his shoulder. He was wearing a large
sombrero and a full beard. He lowered the binoculars
and looked around him at the men who were waiting in
a small draw behind him. They, like him, were wearing
crisscrossed bandoliers. There were five, including himself, who came across the border when they learned that
a range war was brewing between a big gringo rancher
and Jose Luis Fernandez.

Berto Bolanos had no love for Fernandez, and he

hated gringos. He came across the border in pursuit of opportunity. He could attack both sides with impunity, take whatever spoils there were to take, and get back across the border before anyone was the wiser.

Bolanos held up four fingers, indicating how many men were with the wagons. He waved his men after him, and they started toward the little camp.

Will and Gid were quite a distance away when they heard the gunfire. They had no idea what the shooting was about, but they had trained themselves, over the past several years, to always ride to the sound of the guns.

"Let's go!" Will shouted.

"Hey, Will, when we get there, which side will we fight on?" Gid asked as the two men spurred their horses into a gallop.

"We'll figure that out later," Will replied.

"Hell," Gid said with a laugh. "Let's just take on whoever is left!"

It took them four minutes of hard riding to reach the scene. When they crested the hill and looked down below them, they saw four bodies on the ground. The two wagons were being looted. The men who were helping themselves to the contents of the wagons were Mexicans.

"Looks like you had the right idea, Little Brother," Will said. "We'll take on the ones who are left."

While riding with Quantrill, during the war, Will and Gid had often burst onto a scene, totally unexpected. That experience had taught them that boldness and complete surprise could overcome phenomenal odds, even those as great as the odds that faced them now.

Will's first shot took one of the Mexicans out of his saddle before he even knew he was in danger. Gid dropped a second one, and Will got another one with his next shot. Now there were only two Mexicans remaining. The odds were even as far as numbers go, but in boldness and surprise, they had shifted dramatically to Will and Gid.

The remaining Mexicans returned fire, and Will heard a bullet cut the air as it whistled by him. He leaned over the neck of his horse and continued the charge. He hit one of the Mexicans in the knee and heard him cry out in pain. Gid had his hat shot from his head, and the bullet spooked his horse. He kept his saddle and still managed to return fire. The remaining two Mexicans, seeing that they were no match for the charging Americans, spurred their horses into a gallop, abandoning their spoils in their panic. Will and Gid halted at the wagons, and though they fired a few parting shots at the fleeing bandits, they didn't go after them.

Will was the first to dismount and look at the seven men lying in the dirt. The bodies were the four Americans the Mexicans had killed in their attack and the three

Mexicans Will and Gid had shot.

"What's in the wagons?" Gid asked.

Will looked through the load, pushing a few items around.

"Looks like some cloth, washboards, shoeblack, and something called Extract of Buchu Elixir, whatever the hell that is."

"Anything we can use?"

"Apple peelers, ladies' corsets, picture frames," Will went on, reading the labels from the boxes. He sighed and ran his hand through his hair. "Are you telling me that seven men died for a couple of cases of corsets?'" he asked disgustedly. "What a waste."

"Damn," Gid said. "You'd think that, with two wagons, there'd be something worth our stealing."

"All right," Will said. "Let's throw the bodies into the back of the wagons and we'll take them into town."

When the two wagons pulled into town, they got everyone's attention. Gid drove the first wagon, Will drove the second. Their horses were tied on behind, trailing the wagons at a slow walk. Everyone recognized the wagons immediately as belonging to Cooper's Freight Service. But nobody knew who the two men were driving them.

"Wasn't Cooper drivin' one of them wagons when they left out of here?" someone asked.

"He sure was. And Smitty was on the second wagon.

They had McVeigh and Graham with 'em too."

"Well, then, who the hell are these men? They sure as hell didn't go out with the wagons."

A twelve-year-old boy, with a bolder approach to satisfying his curiosity, ran out into the street, his shirt flapping out of his trousers. He trotted up to one of the wagons, then looked inside. When he saw the bodies inside, he started shouting the news to the others.

"It's Mister Cooper!" he yelled. "He's dead an' so's all the others. They's four..." he said before looking back into the second wagon and seeing the bodies of the Mexicans. "No, wait, they's six...seven, they's seven dead men in these wagons. Four American and three Mex!"

"Did you boys kill Cooper, mister?" someone asked Gid.

Gid didn't answer.

From the stores, saloons, cantinas, barbershops, and cafes, citizens of the small town of Carmen, alerted by the boy's words and the shouts of others, came outside to move silently down the street. They kept pace alongside the wagons as the somber procession moved slowly down the street. Finally the wagons reached the center of the plaza where Gid and Will set the brakes then climbed down.

The sheriff came out into the plaza, looked at the seven corpses, then took off his hat and wiped his forehead with a dirty red bandanna.

"Who are they, Sheriff?" someone asked, pointing to the Mexicans.

"I don't recognize them," the sheriff answered. He looked toward the group of brown-skinned citizens who, forming half the population of Carmen, had turned out with equal interest. "Any of you hombres know them?" he asked.

There was a long moment of silence among the Mexicans as they consulted quietly and in their own language with each other. Finally one of them spoke, hesitantly.

"I know one of them."

"You know one, Bruno? Which one? Who is he?" the sheriff asked.

"That one is Hector," Bruno said, pointing to one of the bodies. "He's my cousin."

"I've never seen him before," the sheriff replied. "He doesn't live here in Carmen does he?"

"No, Senor Sheriff," Bruno answered. "He lives in Mexico. He is a bad man, and he rides with Berto Bolanos."

At the mention of Bolanos' name, everyone buzzed with excitement. They had all heard of Berto Bolanos. The bandit had built a reputation for himself south of the border, robbing banks, raiding entire villages, and fighting pitched battles with the Federales.

"I never heard of Bolanos coming over on this side of the border," the sheriff replied. He looked at Will and Gid. "Who are you two fellas?" he asked. "How'd you get involved in this?"

"I'll vouch for them, Sheriff. The mean-looking one is Will Crockett. The big fella is his younger brother Gid," a voice said. It was a voice that Will and Gid had heard before, though not for many years.

A tall man, clean-shaven and with a narrow, pinched face and gunmetal-gray eyes, stepped out of the crowd.

"That's..." Gid started.

"Lieutenant B J Broomfield," Will finished.

Lieutenant Broomfield had ridden with Will and Gid during their time with Quantrill's Raiders. After the raid on Lawrence, Broomfield boasted to the others that he had "sent ten Yankees to their Maker", though as Will and some of the others discussed later, at least half of Broomfield's victims were under sixteen.

"You know these boys, Boss Man?" the sheriff asked.

"I know them. They are fine men, who fought brave-ly for the South during the War Between the States." Broomfield walked over to the wagons and looked at the dead Mexicans. "And I am happy to see that they are still patriots. These Mexicans may be bandits from south of the border, but there's no doubt in my mind why they are here."

"You figure Fernandez brought them?" someone asked.

"Of course he did," Broomfield replied. "He'd do anything to run me out of here...and if he manages to do that, the rest of you may as well learn Spanish, 'cause there won't be any Americans left."

"Now, we don't know that Fernandez brought these men up here," the sheriff said.

"Come on, Sheriff. Is there any doubt at all?" Broomfield asked. "You know damned well we're in a war here. Didn't his men attack one of my line shacks the other night and kill three of my boys?"

"There is no proof that it was Fernandez's men who killed your boys," the sheriff said. "Just like there is no proof that any of your men killed Alfredo Fernandez."

"Yes, well, nevertheless, there's bad blood between High Point and Tularosa," Broomfield said. "But everybody knows that." He nodded toward the wagon. "Now, from the looks of things, Fernandez has arranged for his friend Bolanos to take the war to the folks in town now."

"Senor," Bruno said, "Bolanos is not a friend of Senor de la Fernandez. They have long been *enemigos.* Enemies."

"Yeah, well, they're both Mexicans," Broomfield said. "That's enough for me."

"You can't lump them all together like that. Fernandez has been a good citizen for as long as I've known him," the sheriff said. "And these hombres are Mexican bandits from across the border."

"Yeah? Well, you said it yourself, Sheriff. You never

knew Bolanos to come across the border before now."

The sheriff rubbed his chin and looked at the three dead bandits.

"No," he agreed slowly. "I don't reckon I have."

"Well, there you have it. They came across the border because Fernandez brought 'em across. It don't make no difference to him. All he cares about is stealing as much land as he can grab off. If a few innocent folks get killed along the way, well, so be it. So I don't intend to trust any Mexican."

The sheriff took in the several gathered Mexicans of the town with a wave of his hand. "I don"t agree with you there. Our people have always been a decent enough sort."

"And they will be again, Sheriff, once we let Fernandez know who is in charge around here."

"And just who would you say *is* in charge around here?" the sheriff asked, rather sharply.

"In town, Sheriff, you're in charge," Broomfield said, smiling without humor. "But out of town...on the range...a new day has come. Tularosa is no longer the *'rancho grande',* and Fernandez is no longer the crown prince. Now it's High Point and a man folks call *'El Jefe'.*" Broomfield's smile broadened, and now it was genuine. "You might say, 'The King is dead! Long live the King!'"

Several cheers greeted Broomfield's statement, but Gid and Will noticed that, not only did none of the

Mexicans join in the cheering, but many of them looked around in fear.

"All right, all right!" the sheriff called, holding his hands over his head to call for quiet. "Let's break it up. You folks go on about your business and let the undertaker get about his."

With a last, lingering look, the townspeople, Mexican and American, drifted away.

"Will, Gid," Broomfield invited, "how 'bout you boys come on over to the Americana Saloon and let me buy you a drink, not only for what you did here today, but for old times' sake."

"We're not ones to turn down free drinks," Will said.

Broomfield chuckled. "Didn't think so...leastwise, I didn't remember you as such. And while we're at it, maybe we can discuss a little business."

Chapter Seven

It was very obvious that B. J. Broomfield, or *El Jefe* as everyone called him, was pretty much King of the Walk in Carmen. When he took Will and Gid into the Americana Saloon for drinks, the crowd moved out of the way before him like the sea parting before Moses. He headed for a table in the back of the saloon, and though there were already two people sitting there, they got up and moved when they saw Broomfield coming toward the table.

"You must come here often," Will suggested.

"Often enough. I own it," Broomfield said. "Look around. You see any Mexicans in here?"

Will and Gid looked around and saw only Anglo faces.

"No, I don't guess I do," Will said.

Broomfield laughed. "You ain't going to either. We don't allow 'em in the Americana. I mean, the sons of bitches are all over, everywhere else. So, I figured, why not have at least one place where an American can have a drink in peace, without having to listen to all that Mexican palaver."

"If you own the place, I reckon you can do whatever you please," Will said.

"Damn right I can do what I please. Malcolm!" Broomfield tossed over his shoulder to the bartender. "Bring one of my special bottles. And three glasses."

"Right away, *El Jefe*," the bartender answered.

"I have a question. If hearing Mexican palaver as you call it is so bad, why do you let him call you *El Jefe*?" Gid asked.

"He works for me."

"Malcom as you called the bartender, I can see. But seems to me like just about everyone around here calls you *El Jefe*."

Broomfield chuckled. "Well, I guess it's because more than half the people you're likely to find within a fifty-mile radius of this place *do* work for me," he answered. "The cowboys started calling me that first, and it just sort of took."

"It doesn't look like you've done anything to get them to change," Will said.

"No, why should I? A fella calls me *El Jefe*, right away he knows where he stands, and where I stand. Makes things a lot easier."

"Broomfield, there is no way in hell I'm ever going to call you *El Jefe*," Will said.

This time Broomfield laughed out loud. "No, I reckon not. We went through too much together, you two and I. And I have to tell you, you boys are sure a sight for these sore eyes," Broomfield said. "It's been a long time since I saw any of our comrades in arms. What about you? You ever see any of the old boys anymore?"

"We've run across a few now and then, but not many, and not very often," Will replied.

"'Course, Frank and Jesse James seem to be the ones who have made a name for themselves," Broomfield said. "They, and the Younger brothers. Ever see them?"

"Not since the war," Will said. "And that's been a while."

The bartender arrived with the bottle and Broomfield thanked him, then pulled the cork and poured the three glasses. "Yeah, it has. You know, if you ask me, those boys would be a lot better off getting out of Missouri and starting all over again. It's not all that smart to be too well-known if you're going to be in the outlaw business." Broomfield raised his drink. "To the boys we rode with," he toasted.

"I can drink to that," Will replied, hoisting his own glass.

The three men tossed down their drinks, then Broomfield poured another round. He lifted his drink. "And now, a toast to the finest cavalry leader ever to fork a horse. William Quantrill," he said.

"I must say, you remember the son of a bitch a lot more kindly than I do," Will replied. "But like I said, I'm not one to turn down a drink, even if it has to be to a bastard like Quantrill."

Again, the three men drank.

"Now," Broomfield said, wiping his mouth with the back of his hand, "like I said, let's talk some business."

"What kind of business?" Will asked.

Broomfield smiled. "The kind of business that I know you boys are particularly good at. The kind of business you handled this morning. You're still not ones to back away from a fight, I see."

"We don't go around looking for fights," Will said. "But if one comes along ...we're not backing away from it."

"Well, boys, there's one hell of a fight brewing down here. And if you'd care to join it, it'll be just like old times." Broomfield chuckled. "Only I'll pay you a hell of a lot better'n you ever got scrounging with Quantrill."

"Against the *bandido* they call Bolanos?"

"Hell, no. Bolanos ain't nothing but a two-bit thief," Broomfield said, dismissing the bandit with a snorting sound and a wave of his hand. "No, the one I'm after is Fernandez. Don Jose Luis de la Fernandez. He's the Mex that owns Tularosa."

"That's a ranch? Tularosa?"

"Not just a ranch," Broomfield said. "It's the finest ranch in New Mexico Territory, maybe the finest ranch in the entire Southwest. If I had that ranch and added it to the acreage I already contol...why, by God, boys, there are kingdoms in Europe that aren't as big."

"What about John Sydney Welch and the Red Rock?" Will asked.

Broomfield looked surprised by the question. "What do you know about the Red Rock?"

"I heard there were actually three ranches here. Tularosa, High Point, and the Red Rock."

"Well, you heard wrong," Broomfield said.

"You mean there isn't a Red Rock Ranch?"

"Oh, there's a Red Rock, all right," Broomfield said. "And I don't mind telling you that it's a fine ranch, well laid out, sturdy buildings, proven water wells. But it's not even one fourth the size of High Point, and right now it's no more problem to me than a flea on a horse's ass. But, once I get control of Tularosa, I'll be going after the Red Rock."

"I wish you wouldn't do that," Will said easily.

"What do you mean?"

"Go after the Red Rock."

Broomfield laughed. "What difference does it make to you whether or not I go after John Sydney Welch?"

"Because he's our employer," Will said. "And if you go after him, you're going to have to go through us."

Broomfield looked at the two brothers as if they had suddenly gone crazy. Then, inexplicably, he laughed.

"Well, I'll be damned," he said. "I wouldn't have thought the old coot had it in him. So he's hired himself some guns, huh? And you boys are it? It's a little different from riding under Quantrill's flag, I'll tell you that."

"Some different, I reckon," Will agreed. "But it's what we're going to do."

"Well, then, don't worry about it," Broomfield said. "Welch and I aren't enemies. And of course I'm not going to go up against my old pards. Why, as far as I'm concerned fighting against them that rode with Quantrill would be like committing treason. Anyway, like I said, the Red Rock isn't really a problem. Fernandez is the one I'm going after. I just said that about the Red Rock because sometimes I get caught up in the emotions, just like we did during the war. Well, you boys know how it was at places like Lawrence. I reckon, as we look back on it, all of us did something we'd probably just as soon forget."

"I reckon so."

"Oh, by the way, I've got someone here I'd like you boys to meet. Wait until you see her. She's a Missouri gal and she's something really special."

"She?"

"Her name is Cat and she's my woman."

Will smiled as Broomfield left, then leaned across the table to speak quietly to his brother. "This is a lot easier than I thought it would be. The son of a bitch is doing our work for us."

"How do you want to do this? I mean, how do you want to take her back?"

"We'll give her a chance to come with us on her own," Will said. "If she's willing, we'll just ride out of here today."

"What if she's not willing?"

"It doesn't make any difference whether she's willing or not," Will said resolutely. "We're getting paid to take her, so we'll just take her. Once we get her back to Blaylock, she and he are on their own. If she wants to come back, she's free to do so. We'll have done our part."

"Then what?"

"Then we'll come back down here and earn our pay from Welch."

"We will have, for sure, made an enemy of Broomfield by then," Gid said.

Will snorted. "So what? I didn't like the son of a bitch when we were riding together."

"That's the truth," Gid agreed. "Here they come," he said quietly.

When Broomfield came back down the stairs, he was wearing a large smile. A woman was also descending the stairs behind him, but as he was blocking her from view, neither Will nor Gid could see her that clearly. They could tell, though, that she was tall and willowy, and well-shaped. She was dressed and made-up like the saloon girl she was, with lots of paint on her face, and a dress that looked more like it belonged in a bedroom than on the street. And though she was beginning to show some dissipation from her life on the line, it was obvious that she had been, and was still, a very pretty woman.

"Boys, this little angel is Cat Clay," Broomfield said. "Cat, these two galoots rode with me when I was with Quantrill. I heard Quantrill himself say that these two boys was worth a whole company of men. This here is Will and Gid Crockett."

Cat had kept her eyes down until that point. But when she heard their names, she gasped and looked up at them.

"Gid?" she said. "Gid, is that you?"

Cat's lips were painted a bloodred, her natural features were covered with rouge and mascara, and the hair that framed that face was an unnatural blonde. But there was something strangely familiar in her eyes...deep, cobalt-blue eyes which were now staring so intensely at Gid.

"Have we met?" Gid asked.

Broomfield laughed. "I wouldn't doubt it," he said. "Before I took Cat off the line, she was a whore. She's worked at half the saloons in Texas."

Cat continued to stare at Gid, and though she said nothing, her eyes welled with tears, then they began sliding down her face, cutting a path through the heavy makeup.

"What is it?" Gid asked. He could feel a connection with this woman, and though he didn't know why, he couldn't deny its intensity.

"You didn't come back," Cat said.

Will was still in the dark. "I beg your pardon?" he replied. "Gid, you know this girl?"

"You didn't come back," Cat said again. "I waited for you. I waited for an entire year. I thought, surely, you would write, you would get word to me, someway. But when I heard nothing after all that time, I gave up. I...I thought you were dead."

"Oh, my God," Gid said quietly.

Once, when Gid was very young, he was kicked in the stomach by a mule. No ribs were broken, but his breath had been knocked out of him, and he could remember lying on the ground for a long, agonizing moment, trying to breathe, wondering, in fact, if he would ever breathe again.

He had that same sensation now.

Will still didn't know what was going on, but he knew now that Gid did. He looked into his brother's eyes and saw the most terrible longing for a life that might have been since the time the two of them had stood together over the smoldering ruins of the family farm, many years ago.

"My God, you're Katie Ann," Gid said. His voice was quiet, almost reverent.

Cat nodded, but no words came. She choked back a sob.

Now, as Will looked at Cat Clay, he knew that Gid was right. Gid was first to recognize the young girl who had once been their neighbor, but that could be expected. If there had been no war, if things had gone as planned, this girl would now be Gid's wife, and they would be raising children and running a farm together, back in Missouri.

"Katie Ann McMurtry," Gid said. "God in Heaven, girl, what are you doing here?"

Cat didn't answer. Instead, she whirled around and literally ran back up the stairs.

"Cat! Cat, that's no way for you to be behaving in front of my friends!" Broomfield called. He started toward the foot of the stairs, but Gid reached out and grabbed him by the arm, pulling him back.

"No," Gid said sharply. "Leave her be."

"Look," Broomfield said. "I don't know what all that was about, just now. And the truth is, I don't care. If you know her from somewhere before, that's fine. But she's my woman now, and you'll not be telling me how to handle my woman."

"I said, leave her be," Gid said again, his voice cold and dangerous.

For a long moment the two stared at each other, then

suddenly, Broomfield smiled and nodded.

"All right," he said. "I don't know what's going on here, but I can see that Cat's upset. I'll give her a chance to pull herself together." The smile left his face. "But a word of advice. Don't get any ideas that whatever might have gone on between the two of you before can happen again. Like I said...she is my woman."

In her room upstairs, Cat Clay closed the door and locked it. She stood there for a long moment, staring at the locked door, wishing there was also a door in her heart that she could close and lock.

She was Cat Clay now, Cat, instead of Kate. She chose the last name Clay as a reminder of the county of her birth, Clay County, Missouri.

In truth, she knew that Gid Crockett wasn't dead, and had known it for a long time. She had learned it the first time when she saw some of the early wanted posters on the two brothers.

Will and Gid had attempted, like so many other soldiers of the Confederacy after the war, to turn themselves in for the amnesty program. But amnesty had been denied those who rode with Quantrill. There was a price on their heads, and when they tried to turn themselves in, they were arrested and sentenced to hang. They blasted their way out of a prison train, and from then on, had no choice but to leave Missouri and go on the run.

Cat Clay, or Katie McMurtry as she was known then, waited patiently, for as long as a year, for Gid to come back for her. Realistically, she had known that Missouri was dangerous for him, but she nevertheless clung to the promise he had made to her before the war.

Although she had the door to her past slammed shut in her heart, the memories, as if of their own volition, came flooding back to her.

The white-flagged dogwoods and the lavender red-bud trees were creating beautiful swirls of color in the Missouri hills in the spring of '61. It was the time of the annual Clay County Farmers' barn dance, and Katie, who was eighteen that year, had waited for it throughout the long, bitter winter of '60 and '61.

The barn dance was the first, and the biggest, social event of the season. Katie had been going to them since she was twelve, and she enjoyed the dancing, and the music, and food, and the giggling, girlish conversations with all her friends. But this year she was looking forward to the dance for a different reason. This year, she would be with Gid Crockett.

The Crockett family owned the farm next door to the McMurtrys, and Gid was the youngest of the two Crockett sons. Most of the girls in the county thought that Will was the more handsome of the two, and a lot of girlish fantasies had been built around him.

But Katie was smitten with Gid. She liked his quiet strength and his boyish shyness. She also liked the fact that Gid shared her love of the land and farming.

"Gid Crockett has the makings of a fine farmer," Katie heard her father say one day when he and some other men were in a discussion about the future of Clay County. "Yes, sir, it wouldn't surprise me none if Gid didn't wind up doubling the size of the Crockett farm before he's through."

"What about his brother?" one of the others asked. "Will's older, he'll come into half of the Crockett farm."

"Will? Oh, he's a good man, all right, but he's no farmer, and he'll be the first to tell you that. You want to know what I think? I think that Will will sell out his half of the farm to Gid, then go off on his own, some'eres. Yes, sir, Will Crockett is just the kind that's likely to wind up somewhere down in Texas, or out in Californy, looking for gold or some such thing. Will has a bad case of wantin' to see what's over the next hill. But Gid will be right here the day he dies. Gid is the dependable one."

Katie's father didn't make her choose Gid over Will, but his opinion of Gid certainly validated the choice Katie had already made.

The dance had been as wonderful as all of Katie's girlish dreams had anticipated. Then, toward the end of the dance, Katie and Gid sneaked outside for a breath of fresh air. As they walked away from the brightly lighted barn, down the little hill to the split-rail fence, they could hear the music behind them: the thrum of the guitars, the high keening of the fiddle, the whang of the Jew's harp. And though they couldn't see the colors of the flowers, the night air around them was scented with the smell of the spring blossoms and freshly cut grass. Before them the hills were displayed in soft, night shades of silver and black, silhouetted against the star-dusted sky.

"I got something I want to talk to you about," Gid said.

"My, it sounds serious," Katie teased.

"It is," Gid said. He cleared his throat nervously. "Look. I know you're real young, you're only..."

"I'm seventeen," Katie had interrupted. "That's not young, that's a woman, full grown."

"Your pa says I got to wait another year," Gid said.

"My pa says? You've been talking to my pa?"

"Yes."

"About what? What right have you to talk to my pa about me, without talking to me first?"

"That's just it, Katie Ann," Gid said. "Don't you understand? I got no right to talk to you at all, without I talk to your pa first."

"Gid Crockett, you aren't making a bit of sense," Katie scolded.

Gid cleared his throat and nervously ran his hand through his hair.

"What I'm trying to get around to saying, Katie Ann McMurtry, is that I'm getting of the age to start making some serious plans about my future. And..." Too nervous to go on, Gid stopped in mid-sentence.

"Gid Crockett, are you asking me to marry you?"

"Uh, yeah," Gid mumbled. "That is, I'm going to ask you to marry me if I can get around to the asking."

"When do you plan to get around to the asking?"

"Well, that's what I'm trying to do right now," Gid replied.

"Yes."

"I know it's prob'ly coming as somewhat of a shock to you, I mean me being so busy an' all that you prob'ly don't think I even notice you, but..."

"Yes."

"The thing is, well, Pa says I'm already pulling' my own weight with the farm an' we got plans to add some more acreage..."

"Yes."

"So, well, uh, what with more acreage, there'll be enough room on the place where I can build a house of my own, and I was thinking that maybe down by Duck Creek."

"Gid?"

"That is, if you were..."

"Gid?"

"I mean, well, not until you're eighteen, but maybe then, if..."

"GID!" Katie literally screamed his name at him this time.

"What?" Gid replied, startled by the shout.

"I said, yes, I will marry you!"

Gid smiled, then took her into his arms and kissed her.

"Well, why didn't you tell me so from the beginning so I'd be spared all this hemming and hawing around?" Gid asked.

Katie laughed softly. "I don't know," she said. "I guess I just wanted to hear you say it."

"Katie Ann McMurtry, will you become my wife?" Gid asked seriously. "I mean, when you're eighteen, and your pa's willing to go to church with us, and give you away proper."

"Yes, Gid Crockett. I would be very happy to marry you," Katie said.

The marriage never took place. Instead, the war came, and Jayhawkers from Kansas burned the Crockett farm and murdered Gid's mother and father. In retaliation, Will and Gid joined Quantrill's band and, for four long years, carried on a terrible, bloody, guerrilla war. Throughout the war Katie waited patiently, as she had promised. But Gid never returned.

Katie's own mother and father also died during the war, not brutally as had Gid's parents, but of illness. In the end, it didn't really matter how they died. They were dead all the same. With Katie's parents dead, and with the realization that Gid would not be coming back to her, Katie left Missouri. Somewhere along the way she stopped being Katie Ann McMurtry and became Cat Clay.

In the beginning, Cat tried more conventional ways of earning a living: teaching school, working in a ribbon shop, baking pies. But the work was hard and the pay was little. It was easier than she would have ever imagined to drift into the oldest and most profitable profession.

She made very little notice of the loss of her virginity—it had just happened, and she could no longer even remember who it'd happened with.

Last year, in the town of Afton, she met a man, an accountant named Peter Blaylock. Mr. Blaylock wanted to "take her away from the life". Tired of being on the line, Katie Ann had, for a short while, considered it. But she felt no real love for him, and she realized that his interest in her was more as a reformer than as a lover, so when B. J. Broomfield invited her to come with him, she left, believing that, in the long run, what she was doing was best for her, and for Peter Blaylock.

As it turned out, she felt no love for Broomfield either. Indeed, she wasn't sure she could ever feel love for another man. But at least Broomfield passed no judgments on her, and hadn't even asked her to leave "the life". She had no intention of ever marrying him, but neither did she regret running away with him. And if now and again little thoughts of things that could never be happened to pop up in her mind, they were easy enough to put away.

Whenever Katie felt the need to comfort herself with a fantasy of what might have been, she could still recall the kiss she and Gid had shared on that blossom-scented night before their future was taken from them. There was more passion and more eroticism in that innocent memory than she had experienced with all the men she had been with.

She could have lived with that memory for the rest of her life. She was convinced of that. But now Gid was here, downstairs. And never in her life had she experienced such conflicting emotions. Part of her wept with joy at seeing him again after all these years. But just as big a part of her screamed with the pain of having to come face-to-face with that which had been denied her.

She lay on her bed and cried.

Chapter Eight

Rancho Tularosa

In the middle of the night, a small figure walked fearfully into the darkened bedroom of *el senor de la casa.*

"Senor Fernandez," he whispered loudly. "Senor Fernandez, please wake up."

When Jose Luis opened his eyes he saw his houseboy, Oscar, standing by his bed, a serape wrapped around the underwear he used as pajamas. Oscar's eyes were wide and shining with excitement or fear, or perhaps a little of both. Jose Luis had no idea what time it was, but from the position of the moon he knew it had to be two or three in the morning, certainly an unusual time to be called.

"What is it, Oscar?" Jose Luis asked. "Why have you awakened me at this hour?"

"Please forgive me for disturbing your sleep, *Excelente,* but there is an hombre at the front door with a message for you," Oscar said.

Jose Luis ran his hand through his hair sleepily. "A message for me? Why do you bother me at this hour for a message that you could deliver when I wake in the morning?"

"*Excelente*, he would not give me the message. He insisted that I wake you."

"*He* insisted? A stranger comes in the middle of the night and insists that you awaken *el senor de la casa* and you obey?"

"Forgive me, *Excelente*, I beg of you. But he frightens me."

"I see. And I don't?"

"*Perdon, Excelente*, you are a man of great power and wisdom, but you are also a man of justice and fairness. I did not think you would harm me for waking you in the middle of the night. I feared this man would harm me if I did not wake you."

"Very well," Jose Luis said. He pointed to his robe, an elegant garment of purple silk. The coat of arms of the Fernandez family, a plumed helmet above a lion rampant, was embroidered in gold on the left pocket.

"I must tell you one thing more," Oscar said as he helped Jose Luis into his robe.

"*Si?*"

"The man with the message is a *bandido*. I am sure

he is from one of the bands in Mexico."

Jose Luis looked around sharply. "Are there more *bandidos* with him?" he asked.

"I do not think there are more, *Excelente.* Before I came in to see you I looked through the upstairs window. There is only one horse. I am sure he is alone."

Jose Luis opened the top drawer of the chifforobe and pulled out a small pocket derringer. Charging the two barrels with powder and ball, he slipped the little gun into his pocket. The derringer, he knew, was not accurate beyond a few feet, but within that space its .41 caliber bullet was extremely deadly. He nodded to Oscar.

"All right, let's see what our *bandido* friend wants," he said. He patted his pocket. "And if he is too disagreeable, I have the means to deal with him."

Lamps burned in the hallway and on the stairs so that Jose Luis's way was illuminated. When he reached the landing he stood at the top of the stairs and looked down onto the great room where his visitor stood, holding his fringed sombrero in front of him.

The night intruder seemed visibly impressed with the room, and he stood there, looking at the richly paneled walls, cathedral ceiling, hanging tapestries, heavy furniture, candelabras, and polished lanterns. Jose Luis was glad to see the awe with which the messenger was taking it all in, because it meant that his visitor was a peasant whose normal reaction was to be cowed by wealth and position. He decided to use that to his advantage.

"What do you mean by calling at this hour of the morning?" Jose Luis asked in his most authoritative voice.

The visitor looked around, saw the elegant robe and the commanding presence of the master of the house, and he blanched visibly.

"I beg your forgiveness, *Excelente,*" the visitor said, bowing slightly. "I was sent here by my chief, General Berto Bolanos."

Oscar was correct, Jose Luis thought. He'd said the messenger looked as if he rode with a *bandido* band. Every two-peso bandit in Mexico who could get half a dozen men to follow him called himself a general.

At first Jose Luis started to make a derisive comment about it, then he decided not to. It was obvious that his visitor was impressed by title and position; it wouldn't do to undermine that sense of inferiority, even if it meant acting as if the general deserved the messenger's respect.

"And what is so important that the general wishes to tell me about it at this hour?" Jose Luis asked.

"The general wishes to meet with you, *Excelente.* He asks that you come to Le Tigre Pass. He asks that you do this alone."

"What is the meeting about?"

"I do not know, *Excelente,*" the *bandido* said.

89

Jose Luis ran his hand through his hair. The place Bolanos chose to meet him was very isolated, its approaches easily seen. There was no way Jose Luis could have someone go with him without being seen. If Bolanos wanted to do anything to him, Jose Luis would be helpless to resist.

On the other hand, if he didn't go, Bolanos could attack the ranch, perhaps harm his family. He had enough trouble with High Point. He didn't need to be facing an attack by *bandidos* as well. The best thing would be to see what the man wanted.

"When is this meeting to take place?"

"At mid-morning, *Excelente.*"

"Very well. You may return to the general and tell him I will be there."

"Gracias, Senor Fernandez," the messenger said, bowing respectfully.

The sun was one quarter of the way through its daily sojourn when Jose Luis Fernandez reached Le Tigre Pass. There he saw three men waiting in the shade of an overhanging slab of rock. They came out to meet him.

"Don Jose Luis de la Fernandez, I am General Berto Bolanos, at your service," Berto said. He took off his sombrero and made a sweeping bow.

Jose Luis looked at Berto and at the two men with him. He had never seen anyone as heavily armed as these men were. Between them they had six pistols, three rifles, and three knives. They were also a walking armory of ammunition.

"What can I do for you, General?" Jose Luis asked.

Bolanos smiled broadly when Jose Luis called him general.

"No, no, *Excelente,*" Berto said, wagging his finger back and forth. "It is not what you can do for me, but what I, General Berto Bolanos, can do for you, my countryman. I can help you with your war."

"What war?"

Berto forced a laugh. He looked at the two men who were with him, and they laughed as well—high, insane cackles.

"What war? Ah, you say 'what war' when everyone knows of the war being fought between Rancho Tularosa and the gringo ranch called High Point."

"Why would you want to fight in this war?" Jose Luis asked.

"Because, *Excelente,* I am fired with patriotic zeal when I think of the slaughter of your poor brother. Your brother was a hero who defeated a terrible *bandido* and, in so doing, did me a great personal favor since this *bandido* made claims on a territory that is under my control."

"Perhaps so, but this is a private war."

"No, senor, it is not a private war. It is a war between

my fellow countrymen and the gringos."

"You forget, General, I am also American."

"*Si,* you are *Americano* because of the injustice of history. But your soul is *Mexicano.* And anyway, this war is my war, patriotism or no."

"How is this so?"

"It is my war because of the murder of my men," Berto said. "Three men, innocent travelers who happened upon the dead drivers and guards of two freight wagons, were set upon by gringos who burst upon them like demons from hell, shooting them down without so much as one question. Now, I ask you, *Excelente,* what of my men?"

"*Si,* I have heard of these...innocent...travelers," Jose Luis said, making a derisive sneer of the word "innocent" by setting it apart from the rest of the sentence. "I have heard they killed the wagon men and were stealing the goods when they were set upon by the gringos."

"But this is not true. Do you think my men would steal such things as were in those wagons? Bah!" Berto said, spitting on the ground. "It would shame them...it would shame me, their general, for them to steal washboards and ladies' corsets."

"Perhaps so," Jose Luis agreed, deciding it was better to keep his real opinion to himself. "But whatever happened to your men is of no consequence to the war between Senor Broomfield and myself. I thank you for your kind offer of help, but I will not need it."

"You do not take my offer, even though you know that the *pistoleros* who killed my poor men have gone to work for Broomfield?"

"I have heard that Broomfield offered them a job but they refused," Jose Luis said. "I am told that they are going to work for Senor Welch."

"But it is the same thing. Welch is also a gringo, no? And he owns a ranch...the Red Rock?"

"Rancho Tularosa and the Red Rock Ranch have peacefully coexisted for many years," Jose Luis said. "Senor Welch is not my enemy."

"He is not your enemy, yet he is a gringo, and he has hired two *pistoleros*. I think you may be making a mistake. Once more, I am offering my help."

"And again, General, I thank you for your offer," Jose Luis said. "But I must decline."

Berto's eyes narrowed, and for one long moment Jose Luis thought it was going to become a shoot-out. Then, suddenly and inexplicably, Berto laughed. As before when he laughed, his two companions laughed with him.

"Very well, Don Jose Luis de la Fernandez. Fight the war by yourself. But when you find that things are not as you wish them to be, do not come to me for help. By then it will be too late."

"I understand," Jose Luis said. He turned and walked

to his horse with every muscle in his body twitching. He could almost feel a gun pointed at his back, and he wondered if he would live to mount his horse, or if Berto would shoot him down.

"*Excelente,*" Berto called.

Here it comes, Jose Luis thought, and he bunched the muscles between his shoulders, as if by that action he could stop a bullet.

"*Si?*" he answered without turning around.

"*Vaya con Dios, senor.*"

"*Si, General. Vaya con Dios.*"

Carmen

Although Will and Gid frequently shared a hotel room to save money, when they could afford it they would sometimes take two hotel rooms because, according to Will, Gid's snoring sounded like "a steam-powered sawmill".

Tonight was such a night. After securing a room for each of them and having supper with Will, Gid found a friendly card game and played a few hands. He also had a few beers, but he turned down the offers from the women. It wasn't that he didn't find any of the women attractive. It was just that, seeing Katie Ann McMurtry again for the first time in several years left him in a pensive mood, not a mood conducive to spending the night with a soiled dove. That same sense of melancholy also affected his game, so after four losing hands in a row he said goodbye to the table and walked across the street to the hotel. He waved at the desk clerk, then went upstairs to his room to turn in early.

Once in his room, Gid took off his boots and shirt, then turned the lamp all the way down so that only a faint glimmer emanated from the mantel. He lay on his bed, still wearing his trousers, with his hands laced behind his head, staring morosely into the darkness that had gathered just under the ceiling.

There had been many times over the last several years that memories of the past—and regrets over the present—managed to sneak into his thoughts. Normally he was pretty good about shutting them out, but tonight he couldn't do so.

Where would he be right now, he wondered, if there hadn't been a war?

For one thing, his folks would still be alive. They wouldn't have been murdered if there hadn't been a war. And they hadn't been that old when they were murdered, so Gid was certain they would still be around. He and his pa would, no doubt, be partners in the farm. Will wouldn't be there; Will had already told him he was going to leave as soon as he could bring their mother around to the idea of him going off on his own.

But Gid would still be there. He and his pa would've bought the Holly place. Gid knew Mr. Holly wanted to sell his farm, and it lay right next to the Crockett farm. It was good land too. And it would have almost doubled the size of the Crockett farm. That would have given them a farm that was plenty large enough to support two families.

And Gid would have a family. He would've married Katie Ann McMurtry, probably in the Our Lady of Sorrows Catholic Church, Katie Ann and her family being Catholic. They would have had a couple of kids by now, he was sure of that.

If they had had a boy, Gid would have named him Caleb. He was partial to the name Caleb. He thought it had a good sound...the sound of a man who worked the soil. Caleb would be twelve years old now, plenty old enough to be helping out around the place. Gid was doing a man's work by the time he was twelve.

The second one would be a girl. Gid smiled. A daughter. Imagine him with a daughter. He would let Katie Ann name the girl. Maybe something like Polly. That was a pretty name. He sure hoped Polly would look like Katie Ann. But, then, he was sure she would have.

Gid, Katie Ann, Caleb, and Polly. They'd make a fine-looking family, riding into town in a buckboard.

A family.

It was funny, he thought. It was as if he had an entire

family missing: the son and daughter he never had, grandchildren and a connection to the future that would never be. One hundred, two hundred years from now, the world would be going about its business, wholly populated by the descendants of people he met every day. But there would be nothing of himself in that future. Whatever there was of Gid Crockett, from a thousand generations past to the present, would end with him.

Suddenly, Gid felt a profound sense of sadness, as if the war had killed not only his parents, but his children as well. And with that, all that would have been of him, from now until the end of time.

"Gid?" a voice called, interrupting his reverie. "Gid, are you still awake?"

Gid reached over to turn up the lamp. The room was filled with its subdued glow.

"The door's open, Katie Ann," he said.

The door opened and Katie Ann stepped inside, then pushed the door closed behind her. She stood there for a moment, bathed golden in the wavering flame.

"You were expecting me to come," she said.

"More like hoping you would come."

"I was in my room over the saloon, looking out onto the street," she said. "I saw you walk across the street and go into the hotel, so I...I just took a chance and came on over."

"I'm glad."

"Do you mind if I sit on the edge of the bed?" she asked, crossing the room and sitting down before he could answer.

When she sat on the bed beside him, Gid could see that she wasn't wearing all the makeup she had been wearing when he saw her earlier. The effect was to give her a much softer look—though, without the makeup, he could also tell that the years, and her hard life, were already beginning to take their toll on her. She was barely over thirty, Gid knew, but her face had the lines of a woman of forty or more. But it was her eyes that told the whole story. Her eyes were very old.

Katie Ann was examining Gid as critically as he was examining her, and because Gid was half-naked, Katie had more to look at. She gasped as she saw the many scars and marks on his body. One scar, a long, raised, purple welt, snaked its way from just below the left nipple all the way around to his side. Katie Ann put her fingers on it, very lightly, then traced its length.

"Oh, my," she said. "What a terrible scar. How did you get that?"

"A drunken cowboy in San Angelo," Gid answered. "He tried to carve me up."

"What happened?"

"I shot him," Gid answered easily.

"Gid," Katie Ann said, changing the subject then, "tell me what you are doing here. Why have you and Will come?"

"We've come for you, actually," Gid answered.

"What? You mean you knew I was here?"

"We didn't know that Katie Ann McMurtry was here. But we did know that Cat Clay was here. Cat Clay is the one we have came after."

Now Katie Ann looked confused. "And why is that?" she asked. "I've done nothing wrong that the law should be looking for me."

Gid chuckled. "The law? You really don't know anything about us if you think we are with the law," he said.

"If not the law, then who?"

"Peter Blaylock is paying us to find you and take you back to him."

"Peter!" Katie said. "Sweet Jesus, I'd forgotten all about Peter."

"You may have forgotten him, but he sure hasn't forgotten you. He wants you back. And he wants you to know that he forgives you."

"He forgives me?"

"That's what he said."

Katie Ann's face grew hard. "That's damn big of him."

"Don't be too hard on him. Telling you he forgives you is just his way of letting you know you'd be welcome."

"Well, I can't go back. Not now."

"Don't worry about Broomfield," Gid said. "If you want to go back, I promise you, Broomfield won't be a problem."

"You don't understand. I can't go back," Katie Ann said.

"You mean you like it here?"

"Look at me. Who would want me?"

Gid smiled. "Well, besides Peter Blaylock that is, I could think of someone."

"No," Katie Ann said. She began unbuttoning her dress and as the light exposed her chest, she untied her camisole.

That was when Gid noticed several scabs and sores on her breasts in various degrees of severity.

"What...what is that?" Gid instinctively, reached out to touch one of the oozing pustules.

"Bloomfield gets his pleasure by inflicting pain. This is how he puts out his cigars."

"That son of a bitch," Gid said. "I'll make him pay for what he's done to you if it's the last thing I ever do."

"No, Gid. That won't change anything. I know who I am—what I have become. And right now, I want you to hold me. Let me feel just a little of the love we once had for one another. I know it can never be the way we once were, but for this one moment in time, I want to imagine we are back in Missouri. I want us to be together on the banks of the creek, lying there looking up at the apple blossoms or burying our feet in the sand or making braids out of buckhorn stems. We were both so innocent then, but now I am a whore and by your own account you are an outlaw."

Gid opened his arms, and Katie Ann curled up beside him. He could feel her tears on his bare chest as he fought to control his own emotions.

"Katie Ann." Gid expelled a long breath as he pulled her closer to him.

Chapter Nine

Earlier that same night, Will and Gid had eaten supper together before Gid went up to his room. Supper was steak and beans, the beans liberally seasoned with hot peppers, and washed down with mugs of beer.

"These beans will absolutely set you afire," Gid had said. "But damn if they aren't about the best tasting things I've put in my mouth in quite a while."

Will laughed. "Gid, you've never met any food you didn't find tasty. That's your problem."

Gid smiled sheepishly. "Well now, Big Brother, I reckon you got a point there."

After supper, Gid had listlessly played a few hands of poker then left the saloon and went back to the hotel, telling Will that he was tired and was going to turn in early.

Will decided to stay in the saloon, and he was sitting

at his table nursing a beer when, about ten minutes after Gid left, he saw Katie Ann McMurtry coming down the stairs.

And it really was Katie Ann McMurtry he saw, and not Cat Clay. The woman who came down from the second floor where the women of the bar conducted their "business" then walked through the saloon and on outside, didn't look at all like one of the business girls. She wasn't wearing makeup, nor was she in one of the garish dresses the other saloon girls wore. In fact, she was so plainly dressed that she managed to pass through all the men in the saloon without garnering so much as a sidelong glance from anyone.

For a moment, Will wondered if his brother and Katie Ann had made some arrangement to meet later. But he knew they couldn't have. From the time they found out she was here until just a few moments ago, Gid had not left Will's side. If they had made some sort of arrangement to meet later it would have had to be by way of some silent signal, passed between them.

Will looked across the room to see if Broomfield was anywhere around. He didn't see him, and figured that Broomfield had probably ridden out to his ranch by now.

Will picked up his beer mug and held it out toward the door, the street, and the hotel on the other side of the street. He made a silent and imperceptible toast with the mug.

"Whatever happens between you two tonight," he said under his breath, "I hope it works out right for you."

As Will drank his solitary toast, a man came into the saloon, stood just inside the door for a second, then stepped over to the bar. He moved down to the far end where he could see the whole saloon, and from this vantage point, examined everyone through dark, beady eyes. He was small, wiry, and dark, with a narrow nose and thin lips. He used his left hand to hold his glass while his right hand stayed down beside the handle of his pistol. The pistol, Will noticed, was worn in such a way as to allow for a quick draw.

Of all the people in the saloon, only Will seemed to have actually noticed the man, and he studied him quietly as he drank his beer. He knew that this man was about to kill someone—knew it as clearly as if he had been dressed in a black robe, carrying a reaper and wearing a death's mask.

The batwing doors swung open a moment later, and two men came into the saloon. Both of them looked as if they had been long on the trail, and both of them were wearing badges. They too stood just inside the entrance, looking around the room. One of them had eyes to match his gray hair and mustache. He was the senior deputy. The other was much younger, and from the dark hair and eyes, Will guessed that he was Mexican.

Will saw the lawmen study the room, then he saw their gaze find the man at the other end of the bar. Suddenly their muscles stiffened, and when Will looked at the man at the bar, he realized that this was what he had been waiting for.

"Turner," the older man said. "You're under arrest."

"Arrest for what?"

"I got a witness says you're the one who shot Alfredo Fernandez."

"Hell," Turner said leeringly. "Whoever said it was against the law to shoot a Mexican?"

The saloon patrons laughed at Turner's joke.

"You wanna tell that to the judge up in Lordsburg?"

"Look, Deputy, why don't you just take care of the folks up in your part of the country and leave us alone down here, to work out our own problems?"

"Yeah!" half a dozen other voices chorused. "What's it to you whether or not we kill us a Mexican ever' now 'n' then?"

"I have to take you in. You goin' to come quiet?" the deputy asked.

"I got no argument with you, Deputy," Turner answered. His voice was high then, and grating. In a world without weapons he would have been a pathetic figure among men; but his long, thin fingers, delicate hands, and small, wiry body were perfectly suited for the deadly skills required by a gunman.

"Take off your gun belt," the deputy ordered.

Turner put his drink on the bar, then turned toward the deputy. The younger man stepped several feet to one side while still facing Turner. He bent his knees slightly and held his hand in readiness over his own pistol.

"I don't think I want to take off my gun belt," Turner said.

Will saw the deputy lick his lips nervously. Then he watched the deputy's eyes, the narrowing of the corners, the glint of the pupils, then the resignation. The deputy started for his gun.

Turner was fast as a snake. By the time he had his pistol up, it was spitting a finger of flame six inches from the end of the barrel. It roared a second time, even over the shots fired by the two deputies, and a large cloud of smoke billowed up to temporarily obscure the action. When the smoke drifted up to the ceiling a few seconds later, Turner was still standing, the two deputies were lying dead on the floor.

"Is there anybody in here who ain't ready to say this here was a fair fight?" Turner asked the others, the smoking gun still in his hand.

"Hell, Turner, you want me to say the words for you, I will. We all seen it. They come in lookin' for you, and they forced you into drawin'. It was a fair fight, all right."

"Thought you folks might see it like that," Turner said.

Suddenly Turner realized that Will had been staring quietly at him, and instinctively seemed to know that he had been staring at him ever since he came into the room. He put his gun away, then turned toward Will and pointed at him.

"What about you, mister?" he said. "You willin' to say it was a fair fight?"

"I don't intend to say anything, period," Will answered.

"You been starin' at me ever since I come in here," Turner growled. "What is it you're starin' at?"

"I haven't quite figured that out myself," Will replied.

Turner's eyes blinked as he tried to decipher the meaning of Will's comment. Finally, he either decided that the comment was innocent, or he decided that he didn't want to carry the challenge any farther. With a dismissive shrug of his shoulder, he turned toward the bar.

"I'll have another whiskey," he said.

"Sure thing, Mister Turner," the bartender replied. "Sure thing."

Carmen schoolhouse, the next morning

Caroline Welch dipped a cloth in the bucket of water, then began washing the blackboards in the single-room school-house where she taught. When she learned that her father had hired Will and Gid Crockett, she had tried desperately to talk him out of it. She wanted to keep her father out of any war that might erupt between Tularosa and High Point. She also didn't want Will to stay around any longer. If she admitted to herself, she was very attracted to Will, and she intuitively knew that there could be nothing between the two of them.

If only he were here right now, they could pull the shades and lock the doors. No one would see them, they could do anything, and no one would know.

And then, when Caroline realized the extent of her thoughts, her face flamed in embarrassment and she dipped the cloth in the bucket and began washing the blackboard with renewed vigor.

Caroline was not that kind of woman. She had been intimate with only one man, and that was Jimmy Lacy, the man she thought she would marry. She had given in to his incessant demands for sex before they were married, and two weeks later Johnny was thrown from a horse and killed.

For a long time Caroline carried the guilt of his death in her heart, for she was sure the accident was God's way of punishing the two of them for violating His law.

Then, the other night...oh, what did come over her? She would have given herself to Will if he had asked. But nothing had happened, and when she pulled herself together later that night, she drew comfort from the fact that she and her father would soon be returning to Carmen, and the Red Rock Ranch, and she would never see him again.

Now, much to her chagrin, she learned that, not only had the Crocketts come to Carmen, they had agreed to work for her father...which meant they would be out at the ranch. There was no way she could avoid him now!

"Senorita Welch?"

The disjointed thoughts tumbled through Caroline's mind while she covered the board with broad sweeps, watching the slate grow black under each pass as the white film of chalk was cleaned away.

"Senorita Welch?"

Caroline suddenly realized that someone was calling her name, had actually called her twice, though she had been so lost in her own thoughts that it just now got through to her. She turned toward the sound and saw a beautiful young Mexican girl standing just inside the doorway of the school-house.

"Yes?" Caroline asked. She put the cloth back in the bucket.

"Excuse me, senorita, for interrupting you," the girl

said. "You are the teacher and I know you are *muy* busy."

Caroline laughed and pointed to the blackboard, half-cleaned, half-dusted with chalk. "I'd hardly call this very important. Believe me, it's work that can be interrupted," she said.

"I called your name, but you did not hear me."

"I'm sorry I didn't hear you the first time. I was lost in thought, I'm afraid." She ran her hand through her hair and cleared her throat, then made a motion of invitation with her hand. "Please, come in. What can I do for you, dear?"

The girl came into the room and, at Caroline's suggestion, sat at one of the desks. She looked around the room and smiled. "It is nice, your school," she said.

"Thank you."

"My name is Dona Violetta Maria de Alacon Martinez."

"Heavens, that's quite a name," Caroline teased.

Violetta laughed, her black eyes flashing, then she blushed. "I am told it is proper for one to tell a teacher the full name. I am called Violetta."

Suddenly Caroline realized who Violetta was, and the smile left her face, replaced by a look of concern.

"Oh, you poor child," she said. "You were the fiancé of Senor Fernandez's brother, weren't you?"

"*Si,*" Violetta said. Her eyes darted down quickly. Caroline envied the young girl her lashes, for they were as long and as delicate as a black lace fan.

"I was sorry to hear about that," Caroline said. "I don't know who did it, but I do hope they are caught and punished."

"Please, Senorita Welch, these are bad times," Violetta said. "The *Mexicanos* and the *Norteamericanos* are in... how do you say?...*los campos opuestost?*"

"Opposite camps," Caroline said.

"*Si.* Opposite camps," Violetta said, nodding. "But Senor Fernandez says that your father, Senor Welch, and he are not enemies."

"No, they are not."

Now Violetta smiled broadly. "And so, we are not enemies either, you and I."

Caroline nodded. "I agree. We are not enemies. Now, tell me, Violetta, why are you here? Is there something you want? Something I can do for you?"

"*Si,*" Violetta replied. She folded her hands on the desk in front of her, then drew a deep breath. "I ask to go to your school."

"You?"

"*Si.* I can read and write in my language, and some in English. But I wish to learn more."

"Oh, I don't know," Caroline said. "My students are all much younger... from the first grade until the eighth. I don't even have books for someone of your age."

"Please, Senorita," Violetta interrupted. "I am older, yes, but I do not have much school. My father took me from the school and made me learn many other things... how to act like a lady, how to make lace, how to smile and dance for the men."

Caroline smiled.

"But now I wish to learn things I can use," Violetta continued. "If you say yes, I will work hard for you. I will help you watch over the little ones. I will scrub the blackboard for you. I will carry books, I will..."

Caroline laughed and held up her hand. "Goodness, Violetta, it isn't necessary for you to do all that," she said. "If you wish to attend my school, I will be very happy to have you."

Violetta let out a squeal of delight. "Oh, thank you!"

"Be here tomorrow morning," Caroline said.

"I will be!" Violetta promised. She got up from the desk and hurried to the door, then stopped and looked back. The happy smile on her face was temporarily gone, replaced with a more serious look. "And, Senorita Welch?"

Caroline looked up at her. "Yes?"

"Let us say that here, in this classroom, all of us, *Mexicano* and *Norteamericano,* will be with friends."

Caroline agreed, smiling warmly.

Violetta's face lit up in another smile, then she waved happily and left the building.

Chapter Ten

"We're not taking her back," Gid told Will. "She doesn't want to go, and we aren't going to make her go."

"All right," Will agreed easily.

"That's it?" Gid asked, surprised at Will's easy acquiescence. "You're not going to try an' talk me into it for the rest of the money?"

"Nope."

"What about the fifty dollars Blaylock's already given us?"

"We'll call that expenses," Will said.

Gid smiled. "Yeah," he agreed. "Expenses."

"So, what's going to come of her?" Will asked. "Is she going to stay with Broomfield?"

Gid shook his head. "Not if I can help it," he said.

"Gid, are you going to marry her?"

"I don't know the answer to that question, but the

way she feels right now, I would say no."

"I know that all during the time we were with Quantrill, you had your heart set on going back home, marrying that girl, and taking up farming again. Sometimes, I think I'm the reason you didn't do that. I've thought about that some over the last several years. I want you to know how sorry I am."

"Hell, Will, you weren't the cause," Gid said. "I was a big boy, even back then. If I had wanted to stay in Missouri and farm, I reckon that's what I would have done. The truth is, I guess too many things have happened, and I sort of changed, somewhere along the way."

"You mean, you don't blame me?"

"Never have, never will."

Will's face broke into a big smile. "I'm mighty glad about that," he said. The smile faded. "But that still hasn't answered my question. What happens now?"

"We have to somehow get Broomfield. I'll kill the son of a bitch outright if I meet him on the street," Gid said.

"And how will that help Katie Ann if his henchmen string you up on the town square?" Will asked. "I think I may have another idea."

"What exactly do you have in mind?"

"Seems to me like, with this range war going on between Tularosa and High Point, there's going to be a few cows going back and forth between the ranches. I figure Fernandez will steal from Broomfield, and I know Broomfield will steal from Fernandez, and you can be damn sure they've rustled cows from Welch. Why don't we see to it that more cows get taken from Broomfield?"

"And what do we do do with them? Turn the cows into Welch's herd?" Gid asked.

Will shook his head. "No, that would just draw Welch into the conflict, and it's best that he stays neutral. But last night I overheard some information that might be useful. There's a town across the border called Polomas where the Mexican government has an agent stationed. From what I heard, the agent is buying all the cattle he can get his hands on. I'm thinking I should go down there and see if I can make a deal for some cows."

"Aren't they likely to start asking questions when the High Point brand shows up without having a bill of sale?" Gid asked.

"If they start asking questions, I'll give 'em answers."

"What kind of answers?"

"Why, the kind of answers they will want to hear, Little Brother," Will said easily

Polomas

A dozen adobe structures, baking in the blows of the hot, Mexican sun, framed a plaza where the town's well provided the only water for several miles in all directions.

A few of the citizens saw Will's arrival, watching him with dark, obsidian eyes, staring out from under the large sombreros they wore. Because he arrived in the middle of siesta, however, most didn't even look up, but lay stretched out in what shade they could find to continue their afternoon nap.

Will rode to the well, then pulled up a bucket of water. He satisfied his own craving as his horse slaked its thirst by drinking from the watering trough. When he had drunk his fill, he wet his bandanna and wiped the dust and dirt from his face and neck. Finally, somewhat refreshed from the long, hot ride, he looked around the square until he saw what he was looking for.

One of the low, flat-roofed adobe buildings differed from the others, not in construction or elegance, but only because of the red, white, and green Mexican flag, which hung limply from a pole in front of the building. The building was also guarded by a private in the Mexican army.

Will remounted, rode over to the building, then dismounted and snapped his fingers at the private.

"You, Private," he said irritably. "Is this any way to greet a man who has the endorsement of the leader of your country, *el presidente* Porfirio Diaz? Take care of my horse, at once!"

At the sound of Diaz's name, the soldier moved quickly

to take the reins from one who spoke with such authority. A captain, seeing this, came over to Will.

"I beg your pardon, senor," the captain said. "But who are you and what are you doing here?"

"What am I doing here?" Will asked. He looked around at the sleeping little village, then at the barracks where the troops were billeted. "I am here at the invitation of your government. Now, I have a question for you, *Capitan.* Why wasn't I met by a military escort as the *presidente* promised?"

"I'm sorry, senor," the Mexican captain answered, obviously cowed by Will's demeanor. He spoke in rapid Spanish, and soldiers started running in all directions.

"Where is your *comandante?*" Will demanded.

"Please, senor, this way," the captain said. "I have sent for the colonel."

Will followed the captain into the barracks. The captain showed him into a reception room, surprisingly elegant inside, when compared to the outside of the building. They were met by a white-jacketed orderly and shown to a table. Another orderly poured a glass of brandy for him.

"Well, now," Will said, holding up the glass and letting it catch a sunbeam to explode in a brilliant burst of light, "this is more like it."

The captain and orderlies left Will alone for a few moments and he leaned back in the chair to look around the room. A picture of President Diaz hung on one wall. He saw a humidor of fine cigars on the table, and he took four, putting three of them in his pocket, then biting the tip off the fourth. He looked for a cuspidor and, seeing none, spit the end on the carpet. He had just lit it when the *comandante* breezed in, still buttoning his tunic, exchanging rapid Spanish with the captain who had shown Will in.

"I am Colonel Camilo Palaex, senor," the colonel said, drawing to a stop in front of Will and clicking his heels together ceremoniously. The captain stood at rigid attention behind his colonel, the orderlies behind the captain. "And you are, senor?"

"Ah, yes, Colonel Palaex," Will said, without answering the colonel's question. He examined the end of his cigar for a moment, then held it up. "An excellent cigar, Colonel. But then, *Presidente Diaz* did say you were a man of good taste."

Colonel Palaex beamed proudly. *"El Presidente Diaz* spoke my name?"

"Of course, he did, Colonel," Will said. "When I approached him about the cattle deal I have in mind, he said you were the one to see."

Colonel Palaex saw that Will's brandy glass was nearly empty, and he snapped his fingers at one of the orderlies. The orderly picked up the brandy decanter and Will's snifter was refilled.

"Senor, I am most embarrassed," Colonel Palaex said. "But His Excellency has not contacted me about you. I must confess that I do not know what this is about."

"Of course, he has not contacted you," Will said. "The whole idea was to keep this operation as quiet as possible." Will looked at the others in the room. "So, if you don't mind, could you tell these other men to leave so that you and I may speak alone?"

"Si, senor, at once," Colonel Palaex said. Making an impatient wave of dismissal, Palaex quickly cleared the room.

Will waited until he was certain the others were gone before he spoke.

"Colonel Palaex, do you know a man who lives in Carmen, New Mexico, named Elio Gonzales?"

"Elio Gonzales?" Palaex replied, his face registering curious surprise at the name. *"Si,* he is my cousin."

"Elio sent me to you."

"Elio? Not President Diaz?"

Will shook his head. "No, that was for the benefit of your captain and your men," he said. "What I am about to tell you now is for you only."

"I see," Colonel Palaex said. The tenor of his voice had cooled. "And what is this about?"

"Money, Colonel Palaex," Will said. "A great deal of

money for you, if you are smart. And your cousin says that you are a smart man."

Palaex nodded. "I would not want to accuse my cousin of speaking falsely. Tell me, senor...I still do not know your name, how is this money to be made?"

"Cattle."

"Cattle?"

"You are buying cattle for the Mexican government, aren't you?"

"*Si.*"

"And you are paying twenty-five dollars a head?"

"*Si.*"

"Colonel, I am going to sell you prime beef on the hoof for fifteen dollars a head. You, in turn, will tell your government that it is costing you twenty dollars a head. Your government will be pleased to be getting cattle for five dollars under the going price. They will be saving money, while you will be making money. At five dollars a head, Colonel Palaex, it won't be long until you are a wealthy man."

"And my cousin? What is his percentage?"

"From my share I will give your cousin one dollar per head," Will explained. "You will be able to keep all the money you make for yourself." He smiled. "So you see? We can all profit."

Colonel Palaex did a quick calculation in his head,

then smiled broadly. "Senor, are you certain you can make these cattle available?"

"Absolutely," Will promised. "Are you sure you can come up with the money?"

"*Si.* In two weeks, I will have the payroll for every military person in northern Sonora. I will use money from that payroll to pay for the cattle. Once I have sold the cattle to my government, I will replace the money."

"Sounds like a workable plan to me," Will said.

Palaex poured them each another glass of brandy, then he held his glass up to click it against Will's glass. "To cattle, senor," he said. "And to a profitable business between our two great countries."

Will laughed. "Our countries, hell," he said. "I'm drinking to a profitable business between you and me."

"And what our countries do not know will not hurt them, eh, senor?" Palaex asked.

"Believe me, Colonel, they'll never feel a thing," Will said.

When Will returned to Carmen, he reported on his trip to Gid.

"We've got a deal," he said. "All we need now are a few cows."

"I've already made a start," Gid said.

"How's that?"

"I've found a box canyon out in the mountains. It's open range, nobody uses it. I've already got twenty head of High Point cows in there, and I saw another five head down by the south breaks. We can move those in with no one the wiser."

"Damn! Even counting Gonzales's cut, that's two hundred eighty dollars already," Will said. "You know something? This might turn out to be one of the best deals we've ever run into."

"Wait a minute, Will, before you start counting the money. There's somebody else who deserves a cut as well."

"Katie Ann?"

"Yes, Katie Ann. You don't have any idea what that son of a bitch has done to her. I'd take his whole herd and burn his house down too, if I could," Gid said.

Chapter Eleven

One of the things that made the Red Rock a valuable piece of property was the water that flowed through the place. There hadn't always been a natural flow of water. The creek was little more than a seasonal bayou, a runoff from a larger stream when John Sydney Welch first began ranching. But John Sydney connected the low spots to divert the stream and the result was a year-round supply of water.

Harry Eldredge and Sam Hatten, riders for the Red Rock Ranch, stopped at the stream to let their horses drink, and to dip their hats in the water, then pour the water over themselves to cool down, for it was a hot day and they had been working hard.

Not satisfied to pour water over himself, Harry pulled Sam's collar to one side and poured water down his back.

"Hey, cut that out!" Sam shouted and tossed a hatful of

water at Harry. The two friends played for a moment in the water when one of them suddenly looked up and saw a man on a horse, just watching them. When he realized that he had been seen, he started riding slowly toward them.

"Hey, Harry, who's that?" Sam asked.

Harry wiped his nose with the back of his hand. "I don't know," he said. "But he's sure one ugly son of a bitch."

"Is he workin' for Mister Welch?"

"If he is, I ain't seen 'im before."

"What's your name, mister?" Sam asked when the rider reached them.

"Turner," the rider said.

"Well, Mister Turner, what can we do for you?"

Turner reached behind him and lifted a satchel bag. He tossed it on the ground in front of the two riders.

"That bag is full of blasting powder," Turner said. "What you can do is put it over there, under that rock, then light the fuse."

"What?" Harry asked. He looked over at the rock. "You don't want to do that, Turner. That would cause the whole side of that little hillock there to slide down into the creek."

"Yes," Turner said easily.

"Don't you understand? That would close the creek off. There wouldn't be no water downstream. Cows would start dying of thirst."

"Yes," Turner said again.

"Harry, I don't know who the hell this fella is, but seems to me like that's what he wants to happen."

Turner smiled evilly. "Smart man," he said. "Now, put the blasting powder where I told you to and set off the charge."

"I ain't doin' nothin' of the kind," Sam said. "You can just go to hell, far as I'm concerned."

Turner's face had been totally devoid of expression from the very beginning. He had sat quietly in the saddle, not reacting to anything they said to him. There was no change of expression in his face, nor any abrupt move to give the two boys the slightest hint of what was about to happen. One moment Turner was sitting there quietly, the next instant there was a gun in his hand. He fired twice, and Harry and Sam went down.

Jerome Kelly heard the two gunshots, dry, flat thumps which echoed through the valley. The shots came from the direction of Harry and Sam, and Jerome wondered if the boys had seen a snake.

He chuckled. Sam was deathly afraid of snakes. And he was non-discriminating in his fear. A nonpoisonous snake could generate as much fear as a rattler, and Jerome had once seen him empty his revolver shooting at a garden snake.

Then the smile left his face. There was something ominous-sounding about those two shots, the way they came one right on top of the other. This wasn't the kind of shooting a person would do for target-shooting, or snake-shooting.

Curious, and just a little anxious, Jerome rode toward the stream and the sound of the pistol shots. There was another explosion. This explosion was much louder than the previous gunshots had been. It was heavy sounding, and when the concussion wave rolled across him, Jerome could actually feel it in his stomach.

"What the hell was that?!" Jerome asked aloud, though there was no one but his horse to hear him.

A puff of smoke gushed up from behind the crown of the next hill, formed into a crescent shape, then drifted away.

Jerome spurred his horse into a gallop. When he crested the hill, he saw that the cut through which the stream flowed had been blocked off by half the side of the embankment. Then he saw Harry and Sam, lying on the ground.

"Harry! Sam!"

Arriving on the scene a moment later, he swung down from his horse, then ran over to them. He squatted down over Sam and saw immediately that he was dead. He heard Harry groan, so he left Sam and hurried over to Harry.

"Harry! What happened here? Did you two do this?"

"Turner," Harry said, forcing the words through teeth clenched in pain.

"What?"

"Tu...Tu..." Harry started, then, with a gurgling final breath, he died.

"You killed them?" Broomfield asked when Turner returned to High Point.

"Yes," Turner answered. He walked over to Broomfield's liquor cabinet without being invited and poured himself a drink.

"Anybody see you?"

"No."

"What about the water?"

"I closed it down."

"Ha! Well, it won't take 'em too long to get it open again, but that's not important. The important thing is more'n likely Welch is going to think Fernandez did it. Good job, Turner. Good job."

"Want anything else done?" Turner asked, pouring himself another drink.

"Yes. I want you to go with me."

Turner looked up. "Go with you? Go where?"

"To meet a fella," Broomfield answered.

For some time now, Will had been aware that two men were dogging them, riding parallel with them, and, for the most part, staying out of sight. They were good, but Will was better. He had caught onto them as soon as he and Gid had crossed the border.

They were pushing thirty-five head of cattle south to Polomas, there to meet with Colonel Palaex. Thirty-five head with the Hight Point brand. At fifteen dollars a head that was 525 dollars. After giving Gonzales his thirty-five dollars, Will and Gid had decided they would give all the money to Katie Ann. That way, if she had the opportunity, she could leave Carmen and go anywhere she wanted.

"You see them, Will?" Gid asked quietly.

"Yeah, I've been seeing them for some time now."

"I thought maybe you had."

"Look at the notch in the hill to our left," Will said. "In just a moment, they'll go through there."

Gid looked in the direction indicated by Will and, as Will had indicated, saw the two riders moving quickly through the notch, slipping by so quietly and expertly that only someone who was specifically looking for them would have noticed.

"Who do you think they are?" Gid asked.

"Could be some of Colonel Palaex's men," Will answered. "Or it could be some who ride with Bolanos."

"What do you want to do?" Gid asked.

"Keep the animals moving," Will said. "I'll be back."

Will left the trail and, using a ridgeline for conceal-ment, rode ahead about a thousand yards. He cut over to the gully the two men were following, then dismounted, pulled his rifle from its boot, and climbed onto a rocky ledge to wait for them. He jacked a round into the chamber.

Whoever the men were, Will had to give them credit. They were actually quite good. They approached so skillfully he could barely hear them. Not a word was being spoken, and the rocks which were being disturbed by the horses' hooves were moving as lightly as if they were being dislodged by some mountain creature. Will watched, then saw them come into view from around the bend. He stood up suddenly.

"Caramba!" one of the men exclaimed in a startled shout. His horse reared, and his hand started toward his pistol.

"I wouldn't do that if I was you!" Will warned, raising his rifle to his shoulder.

"Pedro, listen to the gringo!" the other man said. Both riders were wearing large sombreros, colorful serapes, and crossed bandoliers, bristling with shells.

The one who had started toward his pistol stopped his hand, then got his horse under control.

"I don't know what you gents are after," Will said. "But I don't aim to take any chances. I got some money coming to me for these cows, and I don't intend to let a couple of bandits take 'em from me."

"We are not *bandidos,* senor," one of the men said.

"Yeah, well, you're not buyers either, so I don't give a damn who, or what, you are. Like I said, I'm not taking any chances, so drop your guns and belts, then turn around and ride out of here."

"But, senor, there are bandits in this country. It is not safe to be without guns," one of the riders argued.

"You don't say," Will replied. He made an impatient motion with the barrel of his rifle. "I said, shuck 'em."

Grumbling, and protesting their innocence, the two men got rid of their weapons, dropping them onto the rocks with a clatter.

"You know where Polomas is?" Will asked.

"*Si,*" one of the men answered. They were both glaring at Will with open hatred. "We know the village."

"Are you lost, senor?" the other asked. "We will show you the way."

"I know the way," Will said. "I mention it because that's where I'm taking your guns. You'll find 'em with Colonel Palaex."

"Colonel Palaex? Senor, if you give our guns to Colonel Palaex, we will never get them back."

"Colonel Palaex is our enemy," the other said. "He is the enemy of the people."

"Yeah," Will said sarcastically. "And I'm sure you two boys are the friends of the people. Now get."

The two Mexicans turned and started back up the gully. Will fired at a rock very near them and the whining echo of the bullet frightened the horses, or the men, or both, and set them off at a gallop. He waited until they were some distance away, then he picked up their gun belts and draped them across the saddle in front of him.

When he returned to Gid, he saw his brother patiently herding the cows through the remainder of the draw.

"I heard a shot," Gid said. It was more of an observation than a question.

"I hurried them on a bit," Will answered without elaboration.

"Think we can get these cows delivered and be back in Carmen by nightfall?" Gid asked.

"Why, do you have something you want to do?" Will replied. He knew what it was, he was just teasing his brother.

"I thought I might call on Katie Ann," Gid replied, not taking the bait.

"Have you decided what you're going to do yet?" Will asked.

"You mean am I going to take her back to Missouri and start up farming or something like that?"

"Yeah. Are you?"

"I don't know," Gid said. "I'll tell you this, Big Brother. It's tempting. Lord, it's tempting."

"Gid, don't let me hold you back," Will said. "It's not too late for you to make a life for yourself. If you want to do it, do it."

"Hell, Will, you aren't holding me back," Gid said. "I could have left you anytime I wanted before now, you know that. The truth is, I've come to like this way of life pretty much my own self."

"But there could be a lot more," Will replied.

"You mean a wife, kids, settling down?" Gid asked.

"Something like that, yeah."

"I've been thinking hard about that."

"And?"

"Like I told you before, Will. I haven't quite made up my mind. When I do, you'll be the second one to know."

"Second?"

"I intend to tell Katie Ann first, one way or the other," Gid said.

When the wagon pulled into the area between the bunkhouse and the main house, several of the cowboys, drawn by morbid curiosity, came over to look at Harry's and Sam's bodies. Jerome had come back immediately to tell what had happened, then he and Marcellus hitched up a wagon and went out to retrieve the bodies.

"Look," one of the cowboys said quietly. "Hell, last night Harry was sleepin' in a bunk that close to me, I could reach out and touch 'im." The cowboy shivered.

John Sydney Welch was standing by the corral fence.

"What'll we do with 'em now, Mister Welch?" Marcellus asked.

"Do either one of them have relatives anywhere that you boys know of?" John Sydney asked.

"Sam, he has a sister somewhere," one of the cowboys answered. "Think she's back in Georgia or some such place."

"But you don't know for sure?"

"No, sir."

"What about Harry?"

"Harry told me he was raised in a orphanage in Denver. He ain't got no relatives a'tall."

"All right," John Sydney replied. "Marcellus, get them into Carmen and take 'em to the undertaker's. Tell Campbell I said to bury them decent. Nothin' extravagant, but decent."

"Yes, sir."

"Mister Welch, would it be all right if we went into their things and found 'em a clean shirt to be buried in. Don't think they'd like bein' buried like that?"

"Sure," John Sydney replied. "And see if Sam has any letters anywhere. That sister may have written him."

"I doubt that, Mister Welch," Marcellus said.

"Why?"

"Sam couldn't read. Neither could Harry."

"Jerome, did you see who did this?" John Sydney asked.

"No, sir. I just heard the gunshots, then a moment later, I heard the powder go off. By the time I got there, the stream was already closed down and Harry and Sam was just layin' there on the ground."

"And you didn't see anyone?"

"No, sir."

"Did either Harry or Sam say anything before he died?"

"Harry did," Jerome said.

"What did he say?"

"I'm not real sure."

"What did it sound like he said?"

"Sounded like he said...'tough luck'."

John Sydney sighed. "Well, that's not much help."

"One thing good, Mister Welch. Whoever shut down the water didn't do that good of a job," Marcellus said. "I took a look at it while I was out there. Three or four men with shovels can have it open again in no more'n a couple of hours."

"Good. Get some men started on it, will you?"

"Yes, sir. Right away."

As John Sydney walked back to the house, he saw his daughter returning from town in the buckboard.

She could live in town if she wanted to; there was a small house for the teacher, right beside the school. But it was only a couple of miles from the school to the ranch, and one of the concessions she had made to her father in order to accept the job was that she would continue to live at home.

"What is it, Dad? What's going on?" Caroline asked as she stepped down from the buckboard.

"Couple of our men were killed today," John Sydney said. He looked back toward the wagon and saw some men coming out of the bunkhouse with clean shirts. "Harry and Sam."

"Oh, no," Caroline said, putting her hand to her mouth. She knew them. They were both younger than she, and she enjoyed watching them play around, almost as if they were the younger brothers she never had. "Who did it, do you know?"

"No," John Sydney said. "Listen, honey, about your school..."

"What about it?"

"Don't you think that, until all this is settled, it might be best to sort of, well, stop goin' in for a while?"

"You mean just close the school?"

"Yes, if that's what it takes."

Caroline shook her head. "I can't do that, Dad. Those children depend on me. What's happening to them now will affect them for the rest of their lives. I can't abandon them, just because I'm afraid."

John Sydney put his arms around her and pulled her to him.

"All right then, promise me this," he said. "Promise me that you will be very, very careful."

"I will be, Dad. You don't have to worry about that," Caroline said.

Chapter Twelve

Without telling his daughter where he was going, John Sydney Welch rode into the little village of Riata that evening. The sun was down, and the night creatures were calling to each other. A cloud passed over the moon, then moved away, bathing in silver the little town that rose up before him. Although Riata was on American soil, its population was almost one hundred percent Mexican, and one would swear that it was south of the border. Two dozen adobe buildings, half of which spilled yellow light onto the ground out front, faced the town plaza. John Sydney was supposed to meet Berto Bolanos in the cantina. He saw immediately that the cantina wouldn't be hard to find. It was the biggest and most brightly lit building in town.

As John Sydney drew nearer to the town, he could hear someone playing a guitar inside the cantina. It was a mournful sound which caused him to shiver involuntarily. When he was a young boy people used to tell him that such a shiver meant someone had just stepped on his grave. John Sydney put that thought out of his mind.

Stopping his horse just at the edge of town, he ground-hobbled him, then decided to walk the rest of the way, believing that a man afoot would make a quieter entrance than a man on horseback. He didn't want to draw attention.

The smell of beans and spicy beef from one of the houses hung in the night air. A dog barked somewhere, but its bark was quickly silenced by an impatient owner, more interested in quiet than in investigating what caused the dog to bark.

A baby cried.

As John Sydney moved through the little town, slipping between the patches of light and shadow, he thought of the message he had received that afternoon from the man who called himself General Berto Bolanos.

Senor. I have some business to discuss with you, if you will meet me at the cantina in Riata, the message had read.

Because of what had happened earlier in the day with his two riders, John Sydney's first inclination was to discard it. Then he thought there might be a possibility that Bolanos would know something about who killed Harry and Sam. It probably wasn't Bolanos, or he would have never sent the message. More than likely, Bolanos knew who did it, and was going to offer to sell John Sydney the information.

That was all right with John Sydney. If he had to pay to find justice, then he would pay, and do so willingly.

He thought about asking one or both of the Crockett brothers to go with him, then he remembered that they had asked him for a couple of days away from the ranch. He also thought about going to Riata without telling anyone, but finally he decided that wouldn't be too smart. That was why he told Marcellus.

"You're not goin' to meet that Mexican fella, are you, Mister Welch?" his foreman had asked. "Bolanos? Hell, he's the biggest outlaw in these parts."

"Marcellus, I'd make a deal with the devil himself if it meant keepin' either Broomfield and Fernandez from gobblin' up the Red Rock. And you know damned well that business with Harry and Sam today was tied to one of them. I think one of them is tryin' to make me choose sides."

"Yes, sir, I wouldn't be surprised. But it still seems to me that of all the folks we got to deal with around here, the Mexican bandit is the worst. He has to be up to no good, Mister Welch. You just gotta know that."

"You may be right, but there's no way we're ever goin' to know unless I at least meet with him. That's all I'm doin', for now. I'm just meetin' with him to find out what he has on his mind."

"And where is it that you're a-meetin' him?" Marcellus asked.

"At Riata."

"I've heard of that place. Don't know as I ever been there, though," Marcellus said.

"I haven't either," John Sydney said. "It's mostly Mexican, from what I hear, for all that it is on this side of the border."

"Maybe it would be a good idea if I come along," Marcellus suggested. "Let me saddle up and I'll ride in with you."

"No. I think it might be better if I go by myself. I don't know exactly what Bolanos wants, but I'd like to find out, and I'm afraid if anyone comes with me, it might spook him."

Marcellus stroked the stubble on his chin. "I don't know, Mister Welch. I don't much like the idea of that, and I don't think Miss Caroline would either."

"No!" John Sydney said. "Marcellus, you mustn't tell her."

Reluctantly, Marcellus agreed that he would say nothing of John Sydney's plan, and now, as John Sydney picked his way through the dark street of the little village, he was beginning to wonder if, perhaps, he had made a mistake.

He stepped into the middle of a pile of horse dung. His boot slid through the ooze, then he caught the smell of its awakened odor. Cursing silently, he moved over to a porch in front of one of the buildings and raked his boot back and forth on the step, cleaning it as best he could.

That done, he moved on through the shadows until he reached the cantina. He listened to the sounds from inside. The music had stopped and now there was only conversation, Spanish mostly, but then to his surprise, he heard B. R. Broomfield's voice. Looking up and down the street to make certain no one was watching the cantina door, he stepped up onto the board porch and pushed through the hanging, beaded doorway.

Pulling his hat brim low, he headed straight for the bar and positioned himself in the middle of a group of men. The message he had received from Bolanos made no mention of the fact that Broomfield would be there. If he had known that Broomfield was coming, he wouldn't have come. Now that he was here, though, he thought it might be good to know just what was going on before he made his presence known.

Glancing across the room, he spied Broomfield in the far corner, sitting at a table. Across the table from Broomfield was a Mexican, and, from the descriptions he had heard of the man, the Mexican had to be Berto

Bolanos. The two men were talking, and as their conversation was virtually the only one being conducted in English in the entire cantina, the words seemed to rise above the din of Spanish. John Sydney could hear everything they said quite easily.

"We will make a good team, you and I, senor," Bolanos was saying. "You will fight Fernandez above the border, and I will fight him below."

"Yeah, well, the thing is, General, I don't give a shit what happens to Fernandez below the border. As far as I'm concerned, he can own every inch of land between here and Mexico City."

"I see. So you want my men to attack on this side of the border as well. Am I correct, senor?"

"Yes."

"I will do as you ask. But, for this, you must pay well."

"Why should I pay you for fighting him? Won't you be enriching yourself by selling the cattle you steal from Fernandez? Besides, I thought he was your enemy."

"Senor, you must understand that I am a *revolucionario*. I am fighting against Diaz, the dictator of my people. The few cattle I might steal would be to feed my starving people. And to conduct the battle you ask I will need money to buy weapons and food for my soldiers. Also, if I am to fight on this side of the border it will be very dangerous for me, for, although you regard Senor

Fernandez as a Mexican, he is actually an American. And how will it look to the government of your country if I, a general in the Revolutionary Army of Mexico, were to attack a rich American?"

"All right," Broomfield said. "I will pay you, but I have to have something for my money. So, I'll tell you what, I'll give you five dollars for every head of Fernandez cattle you can deliver to me."

"I can get more for the same cattle by taking them across the border and selling them in my country."

"I thought you were only going to take a few cattle across the border so that you can feed your starving people."

"*Si*. But if I take more cattle, I can make more money."

"Yes, but you will still have to get them across the border. It will be much easier for you to sell them to me, at five dollars per head."

"Ten dollars a head," Bolanos said.

"Seven dollars and fifty cents," Broomfield countered. "And if some of the cows have the Three R brand, I won't ask any questions."

"Three R?"

"Yeah, the Red Rock Ranch. If old John Sydney sees a bunch of Mexicans stealing his cows, he's going to think Fernandez's boys are doing' it. And, since he's just hired himself a couple of gunmen, he might just have enough guts to try and go after Fernandez."

Bolanos smiled broadly. "And fight your battle for you, *si*. You are a *muy* smart hombre, senor," he said. He stuck his hand across the table. "Very well, senor, we have a deal."

As the two men were clasping hands, one of Bolanos's men walked across the room and leaned over to whisper something to his leader. Bolanos nodded, then spoke to Broomfield again.

"Senor Broomfield, I have been told that the man of whom we speak is here."

"Welch is here?" Broomfield said. He stood up and looked toward the bar with an angry expression on his face. He saw John Sydney sitting there. "Welch, what are you doing here?"

"Ask the bandit you just made the deal with," Welch replied. "He invited me."

"You invited him?" Broomfield asked.

"*Si*, I invited him."

"Why?"

"I thought you might like to know that he has been stealing your cows and selling them to Colonel Palaex of the Mexican government," Bolanos said.

"What? Why, I'm doin' no such thing!" John Sydney sputtered.

"*Si*, I think you are," Bolanos said. Bolanos turned

to Broomfield. "Two of my men saw Senor Welch's *pistoleros* driving stolen cattle. When they met, the *pistoleros* shot at my men, almost killing them. Later, one of my spies in Polomas sent word that the *pistoleros* had brought thirty-five head of cattle in to sell. They were your cattle, senor."

Broomfield smiled triumphantly at the man who was his neighbor.

He clucked his tongue. "My, my, John Sydney Welch, I would have never thought you had it in you."

"I swear to you, Broomfield, I don't know anythin' about this. All I know is that two of my men were killed this morning, shot down in cold blood, and I thought Bolanos might know who did it."

"The two *pistoleros* Bolanos's men saw with my cows can only be Will and Gid Crockett."

"If it was them, they were actin' without my approval."

"Of course, it would be without your approval," Broomfield said, laughing again. "I've known those two boys for many, many years now. Quantrill himself couldn't control them; what makes you think you could?"

"Then you understand," John Sydney said, breathing a sigh of relief.

"I understand that you shouldn't have brought them in, in the first place," he said. "And I understand that I cannot let you go back to Carmen... not since you now know of the little business arrangement General Bolanos and I have arranged."

"What kind of business?" John Sydney asked. "I don't know what you are talkin' about."

"I think you know what kind of business," Broomfield scoffed. He turned toward the Mexican bandit. "General Bolanos, I'm afraid you made a mistake when you invited this man here. He is a do-gooder. He will go back and tell Fernandez that you and I are making plans against him." Broomfield looked over into the corner and nodded, a barely perceptible move of his head.

"All right," John Sydney admitted. "I did overhear your devilish plan. And I *am* goin' to tell Fernandez about it. But not only Fernandez, I am also goin' to write a letter to the territorial governor and ask him to stop it. What you two are doin' isn't right, Broomfield. You're tryin' to start a range war. You'll turn good men against good men, and you'll bathe this territory in blood."

"That will not concern you."

"What? What do you mean, it won't concern me? Of course, it will. I live here!"

"I intend to take care of that right now," Broomfield said. "Mister Turner," he called over his shoulder. "I have some more business for you."

"Turner? Who is Turner?" John Sydney asked nervously.

"Mister Turner is going to see to it that this little

disagreement you and I are having is settled in my favor."

This was beginning to get out of hand now, and John Sydney looked around nervously. He, Broomfield, and Turner were the only three Anglos in the room. Help seemed unlikely. He had a wild urge to turn and run, but he fought the urge down.

"Mister Welch, I see that you are not wearing a gun. Maybe you'd better get one," Turner said.

"I'm a rancher and a workin' man, Turner," John Sydney replied. "I am not a gunfighter."

"Here, Welch. Take my gun. It's a good one. I carried it when I was with Quantrill."

Broomfield took his gun out and laid it on the bar next to John Sydney.

"It'll do you no good to put that gun there. I don't intend to pick it up."

"Oh, I think you will."

"No, I don't think so," John Sydney said. "You may think this is a Mexican town, but it's not. It's on American soil, and this cantina is full of American citizens. I don't think even you would kill someone in cold blood in front of so many witnesses."

"It won't be in cold blood. You have a gun, so it'll be a fair fight," Turner said.

"Hardly. You've got your pistol in a holster. This gun is lyin' on the bar. That gives you an advantage."

"That's more of an advantage than I gave your two riders this mornin'."

John Sydney felt his stomach turn and the hair stand up on the back of his neck. "That was you?" he said in a quiet voice. "You killed them?"

Turner didn't answer.

"Yes, it was you, wasn't it?" John Sydney said. "How else would you know about it, if you didn't do it? Jerome said Harry's last words were 'tough luck'. But I can see it now. That isn't what he said. What he said was, 'Turner'."

Turner smiled evilly. "And so now you can see that I mean business," he said. "Go ahead, Mister Welch. Try me. Don't you want revenge? I'll let you wrap your hand around the handle. I won't even start my draw till then."

"No. I won't fight you."

"You're a coward."

"I am not a coward, but I am a prudent man. I have no intention of gettin' into a gunfight here and now."

"What's it going to take to make a man out of you?" Turner asked. Then he smiled again, this smile even more evil than the previous one. "Maybe if I tell you about your daughter...and how I..."

"Leave Caroline out of this," John Sydney said.

Turner's smile broadened. He had found a way to get to John Sydney now, a way, at last, to force him into a shooting match.

"Maybe you want to stay around a little longer so you can watch me have your daughter. She wants me, Welch. I've seen the way she looks at me. I've seen that hungry look in women's eyes before. She wants what I've got for her." He reached around with his left hand and grabbed himself.

"Shut up, you foulmouthed bastard."

"Well, now, Welch. You can shut me up if you want to. You can shut me up and protect that little girl of yours at the same time. If you get lucky, just real lucky, you might..."

Suddenly, desperately, John Sydney made a clawing grab for the pistol. Turner drew his gun and had it pointed at John Sydney before the rancher could even lift the pistol from the bar. Turner stopped and smiled. For just a moment the two men formed a bizarre tableau, then Turner pulled the trigger.

The bullet caught John Sydney in the throat, and he dropped the gun unfired, then clutched at his neck. Blood spilled between his fingers as he let out his gurgling death rattle. He fell against the bar, then slid down, dead before he reached the floor.

The patrons of the bar who had moved out of the way at the start of the confrontation now began moving carefully back to the bar. All of them looked at the prostrate form of John Sydney Welch, his sightless eyes open, his mouth in a grimace of anger, the gaping wound in his throat oozing red with blood. His arms were lying to either side, his hands calloused from a lifetime of work.

A dozen or more of the patrons crossed themselves and a few mumbled a prayer for him.

Chapter Thirteen

Back in Carmen in time for supper, Will and Gid had a good meal in the restaurant, then went over to the Americana Saloon for a few beers. "A few beers" was what Gid said they were going for, but Will wasn't fooled in the least. He knew that what Gid really wanted was to go upstairs to visit Katie Ann. He was happy for Gid and he wished he could see Katie Ann's reaction when Gid gave her the money they had received from Colonel Palaex.

Will thought of Caroline Welch. A couple of times since he and Gid had arrived in Carmen, he had walked down to the school, but Caroline Welch was very distant to him. Why was she avoiding him now?

Whatever the reason, she had made it very plain that she didn't want anything to do with him, so if he was looking for female companionship, he would just have to look somewhere else.

And this was as good a place as any to start, he thought. There were four soiled doves who worked the trade at the Americana Saloon. Actually for Will's purposes, there were only three, because he couldn't count Katie Ann McMurtry. She had pulled herself "off the line". And anyway she was, for now at least, the exclusive property of Will's brother Gid. The two brothers had learned, long ago, never to let any woman come between them.

But that left Will on the prowl. And the pickings seemed exceptionally slim tonight. Two of the Americana working girls had already gone upstairs for the night. The one remaining girl didn't appeal to Will, though she did try to interest him in what she had to offer.

Feeling somewhat abandoned, Will was standing at the bar, nursing a beer.

"She ain't much," the man next to him said.

"What's that?"

"Leonora."

"Who's Leonora?"

"The whore who just tried to get you to take her upstairs a minute ago," the man said. "She's so ugly she'd make a train take four miles of dirt road. She ain't exactly the kind of woman a man wants to belly up to, 'lessen it's been a long, dry spell."

"Don't really like to call any woman ugly," Will said, raising his beer mug to his lips. "But seeing someone like that does make you wonder why she got into the business in the first place."

"Lola," the man said.

"I beg your pardon?"

"You should try Lola. She's a looker."

Will looked around the saloon. "I don't see any other woman in here."

"No, and you ain't goin' to either. Leastwise, not in here. You see, Lola's Mex, and Broomfield, he don't allow no Mexicans in here."

"I see."

"You'll find Lola down the street in the Mex cantina."

"You say she works the cantina?"

"Yes."

"Are you telling me the Mexicans are a little more open-minded about it? They let Americans come into their place?"

"They don't like us any more than we like them, I have to say," the man said. He smiled. "But they do like our money."

Will finished his beer, then wiped his mouth with the back of his hand. He looked upstairs in the direction his brother had gone half an hour earlier.

"All right," Will said. "All right, I think I might just

give this Lola a try."

"You ain't goin' to regret it, I'll promise you that," the man called after Will, as he pushed his way through the set of double-swinging batwing doors.

Down the street in the Mexican cantina, Lola looked particularly alluring this evening. She had black flashing eyes, ruby lips, and teeth as white as pearls. Her long, black hair was tied back with a red ribbon, which matched the color of the sash at her waist. The dress she was wearing was very low-cut and particularly revealing, so when she served Will his drink and leaned over his table, she treated him to a more than generous view of her breasts.

With all the skills of her profession, Lola engaged Will in the art of seduction, running her fingers along his jawline, brushing her hips against his arm. Within a few more visits to his table, aided by a little squeeze here and a tiny pressure there, she accomplished what she set out to do. Will made the suggestion, she quoted a price, and the two of them went up the stairs together. About halfway up the stairs he glanced over at the bar and caught a glimpse of the man he had met in the Americana Saloon. The man held out his glass of tequila in silent salute and Will nodded down at him.

When they reached the top of the stairs, Lola called out in Spanish, and a short, heavyset woman hurried down the hall. She opened the door, then stepped away from it.

"Senor," Lola said, holding her arm toward the open door, smiling in broad invitation.

"Where I come from, it's ladies first," Will said.

"You are a fine gentleman," Lola replied, stepping into the room ahead of him. Will followed her and once inside saw a bed, bedside table, chair, and chifforobe. The heavyset woman Lola had spoken to hurried over to the chifforobe, where there was a pitcher, bowl, and towel. She filled the bowl with water from the pitcher, then turned and started to back out of the room. Just before she left, Lola said something else to her. The woman's eyes grew wide for an instant, then Lola spoke again, more sharply this time, and the woman nodded.

"*Si, senorita,*" she said very quietly.

"Is something wrong?" Will asked, surprised by the sharpness of the words he couldn't understand.

"Delfina is a stupid woman," Lola said. "Every time, I give her instructions, and every time she does not obey."

"Maybe I'd better..." Will started to say, but Lola reached up to touch him.

"No," she said, shaking her head and pouting as she began removing her blouse. "It is nothing." She put her fingers on his neck and Will wondered how they could be so cool to the touch, yet so fire his blood.

"Close your eyes," Lola ordered.

"Why?"

"I have a surprise for you. Here, close your eyes and I will kiss them for you."

Will closed his eyes and felt her lips against the eyelids, first one, then the other. He was drifting in a sea of pleasure.

Then he heard the metallic click as the sear engaged the cylinder and the hammer came back. He felt something cold and hard, and when he opened his eyes, he saw that the girl was holding a revolver pointed at his stomach.

"Do not move, senor," she said in a low, flat voice. All the warmth was gone now.

"What the hell is this? What are you doing?"

"Mario!" the girl called.

The door opened and four men entered the little room. They were all Mexican, and all were smiling.

"Good evening, Senor Crockett," one of them said. He sat on the chair and folded his arms across his chest. The other men began tying Will to the bed. They used leather thongs to secure his wrists to the headboard and his ankles to the footboard.

"Who are you?" Will asked. "What's going on here?"

"Allow me to introduce myself, senor. I am Mario Armijo. I have the honor of being a vaquero for Don Jose Luis de la Fernandez. These men too are vaqueros for Senor Fernandez. You are one of the men Senor Welch hired, no? *Pistolero?"*

"What the hell business is it of yours?" Will replied.

"I know it is true, senor, so please answer my questions. If you do not, I believe my sister would be most happy to shoot you."

"Your sister?" Will asked in surprise. "Are you telling me that you let your sister parade around here, half naked in front of these men?"

Mario shrugged his shoulders and turned the palms of his hands out. "What can I say, senor? My sister is *a puta*. These men have all known her."

"It is too bad we did not get the chance, senor," Lola said. "I think I would have liked it."

"That's enough, Lola," Mario said. "You leave. We will deal with the gringo."

"Do not hurt him too much, my brother," Lola said, smiling as she began putting her blouse on. "He is too pretty to hurt too much."

"Now you will talk to me," Mario said, after his sister left. "You are one of the men Senor Welch hired, yes?"

"Yes."

"But you and your brother. You are not cowboys. You are men who are skilled with guns. You are *pistoleros,* yes?"

"Why are you asking the questions? You seem to know all the answers already."

"Si. I know all the answers, and I think Senor Welch

hired you to help *El Jefe* make war against Don Jose Luis de la Fernandez and Rancho Tularosa."

"I'm damn sure not working for Broomfield," Will started, but before he could finish his protest, a fist slammed into his face.

Across the street at that very moment, Gid was telling Katie Ann McMurtry goodbye.

"I don't know where you got this money, Gid, but I will always be grateful to you and Will. I'm glad you came by tonight," Katie said.

"You didn't think I wouldn't be here, did you? As long as you are here, just try and keep me away," Gid replied.

"He will, you know."

Gid nodded. "You're talking about Broomfield," he said. "Well, Broomfield might try, but trying and doing are two different things."

"Please be very careful tonight, Gid," Katie Ann said. "I don't know what it is, but something is in the air, and I'm frightened for you. People say the Mexicans are all stirred up over the killings that have been happening."

"Don't waste your time being frightened for me," Gid said, as he kissed Katie Ann on the nose. "Will and I can take care of ourselves."

"I know, but this is different."

When Gid got downstairs, he looked around for his brother, but Will was nowhere to be found. He ordered a drink and nursed it for a few minutes, glancing, often, toward the head of the stairs.

Finally, he asked the bartender, "How long's my brother been up there?"

"Your brother? He ain't up there."

"He's not? Where is he?"

"You might try the cantina down the street. Seems to me like I heard him and another fella talkin' about some girl named Lola. Said she was a hell of a lot better'n Leonora over there."

"The cantina?"

"Yeah, you know, the Mexican place."

"All right, thanks," Gid said, heading out into the dark. A moment later, he pushed through the hanging, clacking beads to go into the cantina. When he asked the bartender, the bartender nodded toward a pretty Mexican girl who was sitting at a table near the back wall.

"I am Lola, senor," the girl said, smiling prettily at him when he went over to her. She leaned over to show her ample cleavage. "Can I do something for you?"

"Senorita, I'm looking for my brother. I'm told he may have come in here. Have you seen him?" He described him to her.

"No, I don't think so, senor."

"The bartender said you went upstairs with him."

The girl smiled. *"Si,* I did go upstairs with a gringo. I did not know he was your brother."

"Well, where is he now?"

"I do not know, senor. He has left."

"That's funny. He wouldn't have left here without coming back over to get me. You sure he left?"

"Si, senor, I am sure."

"Yeah, like you were sure he hadn't been here in the first place," Gid said. He took one more look toward the head of the stairs, then turned to leave.

"All right, thanks," Gid said. "I guess I've made a mistake. I'll—" He stopped in mid-sentence, then went over to another table where he picked up a very familiar black hat. "This belongs to my brother," he said. "What's it doing here?"

"You are mistaken, senor," Lola said. "That hat has been here for a very long time."

"You're lying," Gid said. "I think I'll just take a look upstairs."

"No!" the girl screamed at the top of her lungs, moving toward the stairs on the run. "Mario!" she yelled. She tried to block Gid, but he pushed her aside.

Just as Gid reached the top of the stairs, the first door opened, and a Mexican looked out. Quickly, the Mexican slammed the door and Gid heard a key turning in the lock.

Gid didn't know if this was a shy customer with one of the saloon girls, or if Will was in that room, but he didn't wait to think about it. He raised his foot and kicked in the door. The door, hinges and frame, exploded into the room with a puff of dust from the mud-chinked walls. The Mexican who had closed the door wound up on his backside on the floor.

"Dios!" someone in the room shouted, and Gid saw him start for a pistol that was lying on the bedside table. Gid reached the table in one giant step. The man grabbed the gun before Gid did, but he never got the chance to use it. Gid picked him up and threw him through the window. The window smashed with a shower of glass, and the man, with the gun still in his hand, began firing shots into the air and screaming as he fell two stories to the ground below.

There were three other men in the room, and they all started for Gid, thinking to rush him all at once. Gid picked one up and threw him against the wall. The other two turned tail, making for the door at the same time. Unfortunately for them, even with the opening enlarged by Gid's entrance, it wasn't possible for them both to exit simultaneously, until Gid helped them. Bending over to use his head and shoulders as a battering ram, Gid charged across the room at them, roaring like an angry bull. He smashed into them from the rear, popping them through the opening. Both men went flying out into the hall, then flipped over the rail and crashed onto the tables below.

Now everyone in the cantina knew what was going on. Frightened for their own safety, they had left the bar and tables and were now gathered near the front door. Some had already moved into the street, but a few, whose curiosity overcame their fear, stayed just inside and watched as the two came flying off the upstairs landing to crash onto the tables below.

Gid hurried back into the room where he saw Will tied to the bed. Will's eyes were black, his lips were swollen, and there were bruises and scars on his cheeks where he had been beaten. Despite all that, he was smiling broadly at his brother.

"My God, Will, what the hell are you doing here?"

"Whooee, Gid, you do push folks around a mite when you get pissed off," Will said.

Gid cut the leather thongs that bound Will to the bed, then as Will pulled his shirt back on, Gid gave vent to the rest of his anger. He moved down the hallway, kicking in every door to every room, some of which were occupied by terrified girls and their cowering customers. Then, when Gid got downstairs, he picked up a man who was just now getting to his feet and hurled him through the front window.

Scores of people from the other cantinas, and even from

the Americana Saloon, had joined the growing crowd in the street, watching what was going on. Will, who had gone after their horses, rode up, leading Gid's animal.

With the sound of smashing and crashing over, an unearthly quiet settled on the street. No one said a word as Gid mounted, and even as they started riding away, the town remained silent, as if the slightest sound might cause Gid to come after them.

Will twisted around in his saddle and looked back at the crowd and the damaged saloon. He chuckled.

"What is it?" Gid asked.

"Seems to me like you haven't done that much damage in a long time," Will said. "Little Brother, remind me never to get on your bad side."

Chapter Fourteen

One of the advantages of working for the Red Rock Ranch was the fact that Will and Gid had a free place to stay. They were living in the bunkhouse, but, unlike the cowboys who were working there, and who had to get up at the crack of dawn to tend to their tasks, Will and Gid were pretty much free to come and go at will. So, when they returned to the bunkhouse that night, the darkness was rent with the snoring of half a dozen cowboys, long since gone to bed.

One of them woke up.

"You fellas just gettin' in?" Marcellus asked.

"Yeah," Gid answered.

"Wish you'd been here earlier."

"Why? Did something happen?"

"No. Leastwise, I don't think anything has. But Mister Welch went down to Riata, and he ain't come back yet. I'm a mite worried about him."

"What'd he go there for?"

"To meet with Bolanos."

"Bolanos? The *bandido?* The one we ran into when he tried to take the freight wagons?"

"That's the one," Marcellus said. "I wish you two had been here. You coulda maybe gone with him."

"Sorry," Gid said. "We didn't know he had something like that planned."

"It wasn't. He just got the message this afternoon. I tried to talk him into lettin' me go with him, but he wouldn't hear of it."

Gid lit a lantern.

"What'd you light that lamp for?" Marcellus asked. "You goin' to wake the boys up."

"Hell, Marcellus," a voice grumbled from the darkness. "All your palaverin' has already done that."

A couple of others chuckled.

"Sorry, fellas," Gid said. "But my brother is some hurt, and I thought I'd take a look at him."

"Hurt?" Marcellus said. He got out of bed and came over to them. "Let me see."

A couple of the other cowboys left their bunks as well, and they stood on the wide-plank floor, scratching themselves through their underwear as they gathered around for a closer look.

"Holy shit! Look at that!" one of them said. "Damn if you don't look like you was kicked in the face by a mule."

"What happened?"

"I got beat up," Will answered. He was actually laughing.

"You got beat up that bad, and you're laughing about it?"

"Yeah," Will said. "Well, it was kind of funny, when you think about it."

"Who done it?"

Gid poured some whiskey onto a handkerchief, then started doctoring one of his brother's cuts. The whiskey burned, and Will jerked back.

"Ouch!" he said. "That burns."

"It's good for you."

"That's what you say. It seems to me a hell of a waste of good whiskey," Will complained.

"Go on, tell us what happened."

"Well, I went into this Mexican cantina, you know the one, down the street from the Americana Saloon? Say, fellas, they got the best-looking Mexican gal working there you ever saw in your life. Her name is Lola."

"Hold still!" Gid ordered, irritated by the fact that Will was moving his head from side to side while he was talking.

"You tryin' to tell us some Mexican gal did this to

you?" Marcellus asked.

"Lola? No, all she did was hold a gun on me," Will said. "Her brother and some of his friends did this."

Gradually, as Gid doctored his brother, cleaning the cuts and tending to the bruises, Will managed to tell the story, sometimes getting up from his chair to add embellishments, only to be pushed back down by his brother. The story was full of self-deprecating humor and, by the time he was finished, the entire bunkhouse was laughing out loud.

"And all the while Gid was whipping ass, there I was, tied to the bed, and watching it all," Will concluded. "I tell you, boys, I had the best seat in the house."

"Damn me, I wish I woulda been there!" one of the cowboys said. "I would have loved to have seen them Mexicans get whupped by ole Gid here."

"Hey, fellas!" one of the cowboys said, interrupting the conversation. He had moved to a window and was now looking outside. "They's someone comin'!"

"It must be Mister Welch," Marcellus said. "Good, I been some worried about him."

"It ain't Mister Welch. There's two of 'em, and they're leadin' a horse behind 'em. They look like Mexicans."

"What's that?"

"Two Mexicans, leadin' a third horse."

The cowboys all grabbed their pistols, then stepped

out onto the porch. All but Gid and Will were in their underwear, having just gotten out of bed.

"You hombres hold on there!" Marcellus shouted in a loud, demanding voice.

The Mexicans had not yet noticed the cowboys, and Marcellus's booming shout in the night startled them.

"Caramba!" one of them shouted. "Senor, don't shoot! We are but peons!" He and the other rider put their hands in the air and stopped. Their shaking arms indicated their fright.

"What are you two hombres doin' here?" Marcellus asked.

"Is this the rancho of Senor Welch?" one of the men asked.

"Yes."

"I am *muy* sorry, senor," the Mexican said. He gestured with the thumb of his raised hand toward the horse he was leading. "But we have brought you something that is very sad."

"You better make yourself clear, real fast," Marcellus said.

"We have brought Senor Welch to you."

"What do you mean, you have brought him to us?"

"He is *muerto,* senor."

"Muerto? What, do you mean dead?" more than one voice replied.

"*Si.*"

Gid and Will walked back to the led horse to have a look. Marcellus and the others did as well, but they were barefooted, and they had to pick their way gingerly across the rock-strewn ground, so that the two brothers were already there examining the body by the time they arrived.

Will lifted the head of the body so he could see the face.

"Is it him?" Marcellus asked.

Will nodded his head. "Yeah, it's him, all right."

Marcellus cocked his pistol, and the metallic click was loud in the night.

"You boys do this?" he asked.

"No, *senor!*" one of the two men answered. "He was killed by a *Norteamericano*...one of your own countrymen."

"You're lying. He went to meet with Bolanos."

"*Si.* He met with the general. But Bolanos did not kill him."

"Who did?"

"*I told you. A Norteamericano.*"

"Do you know a name?"

The two Mexicans conferred for a moment, as if trying to agree on the name, then they nodded, and the spokesman spoke.

"He say his name is Turner."

"Turner?" Gid said. "Say, Will, isn't he the one who killed those two deputies?"

"That's the one," Will said.

"I knew I didn't like that son of a bitch the first time I saw him," Gid replied.

"Put your hands down," Will said when he noticed that the two Mexicans were still holding their hands up.

"*Si, senor. Gracias.*"

"And *gracias* to you for bringing him back."

The two nodded, then started to turn their horses.

"Wait a minute," Marcellus called.

The two Mexicans halted.

"It's a long ride back and it's late," Marcellus said. "If you folks want to, you can spend the night here."

"You got no call askin' 'em to stay here, Marcellus," one of the cowboys protested. "Where at are they goin' to sleep?"

"They'll sleep in the bunkhouse with us. We got some bunks ain't bein' used."

"No, sirree. I ain't goin' to sleep in the bunkhouse with no Mexicans."

Marcellus glared at the cowboy. "Then you can, by God, sleep in the barn," he said. "Because these two is sleepin' in the bunkhouse!"

"Who's goin' to tell the girl about her pa?" someone asked.

Marcellus took a deep breath. "I'm not lookin' forward to it," he said. "But I've know'd her since she was a young girl, so I reckon I'm the one to do it."

The morning sun was an orange ball, just clearing the eastern range of the mountains. Tentacles of light reached down into the notches of Red Rock Escarpment, clearing away the morning haze which hung in the nooks and crannies like drifting smoke. The red sandy loam was dotted with cottonwood and mesquite, limned in gold from the rising sun.

Caroline Welch, who had not gone back to sleep after Marcellus gave her the awful news last night, came riding onto the scene. Her horse picked its way along the familiar rim line to look out over the sweeping grandeur of the Red Rock Ranch. She rode carefully along a trail that led to a private place, a secret glen she had discovered in her youth, and to which she often came when troubled or when she wanted to be alone, just to think.

She had come up here fifteen years ago, when her mother died, and, as she said her private goodbye to her mother, she knew, even then, that the day would come when she would return for the same reason for her father. And she was prepared for that eventuality; she just wasn't ready for it to happen so soon.

Once on top, she rode out onto the precipice from

which she could see the entire canyon floor and the ranch, including the main house, the barn, and the bunkhouse where the hands slept when they weren't out on the range or in one of the line shacks.

From here too she could see the road that led into the canyon and she saw that, already, carriages, buckboards, and wagons were making their way down the road from Carmen. Word of her father's death had spread like wildfire during the night, and already his many friends were coming to pay their respects.

"Caroline?"

Caroline was startled to hear her name called, for she didn't realize anyone had followed her up here. Ordinarily, she would have also been a little resentful, for this was her own, private place, and she wasn't prepared to share it with anyone else.

But the situation was different this morning. She had come up here, thinking to tell her father goodbye, believing that she wanted solitude for the task. However, once here, she realized how alone, and how lonely, she was really going to be. So when she saw Will coming toward her, she felt glad.

"Oh, Will," she sobbed. She started toward him and Will dismounted and took her in his arms. They stood that way for a long moment, with Will holding her close to him.

It was not hard for Will to imagine Caroline's sorrow. He could well remember how he had felt when he and Gid had come back from a simple trip to buy feed and seed to find both their parents murdered and the buildings of the farm burned to the ground. But Will said nothing of this, for he knew that telling her of his own sorrow wouldn't make her pain any less.

Finally, he felt her move away slightly, and he let her go. She walked over to sit down on a flat rock, choosing her place easily and without looking. Will knew, without having to be told, that this was a place as familiar to her as the living room in the house below.

"I hope all of the schoolchildren got word of what happened," she finally said. "I wouldn't want to think about them showing up for school today without me being there. I hope they all know there won't be any school."

"I'm sure they got word," Will said. He pointed toward the road that led into the ranch. "Everyone knows about it. As you can see, folks are already coming out to pay their respects."

"Yes," Caroline said. "I am pleased to know that my father had so many friends."

They were quiet for a long moment, then Caroline spoke again.

"I'm sorry," she said.

Will looked at her in surprise. "You're sorry? About

what?"

"About you and me," Caroline said. "About the way I have treated you since you got here."

"Don't worry about it."

"No, no, I want to worry about it," Caroline said. "I want you to understand why."

"All right, you can tell me about it if you want to. I'll listen," Will said easily.

Caroline ran her hand through her hair as she paused for a moment to form just the right words.

"It's just that I have painted this picture of myself, all these years, of being a good woman," she began. "I admit that I lost my innocence with Jimmy Lacy. But Jimmy and I were engaged, and I thought that, somehow, God would understand, and forgive me. But God didn't forgive me, and because of my sin, Jimmy was killed when a horse threw him.

"Then you came here and I, I wanted you. Now, God has punished me again. This time he took my father from me."

"Listen to me, Caroline Welch," Will said. His opening words were gruff, but when he saw a tear sliding down her cheek, he softened his tone, and he reached out to catch the tear with the tip of his finger. "I've never known anyone more innocent than you. And God didn't take your father from you. A man named Turner did.

And Turner is the one who is going to have to answer to God." And me, he added silently.

Caroline smiled through her tears. "You're a good man, Will Crockett, trying to comfort me like this."

"I'm not the only one wanting to comfort you," Will said. He pointed to the house, where by now several conveyances were parked, the teams placidly munching grass. "Looks like you have quite a crowd gathered now. Maybe you'd better go down there and greet them."

Caroline wiped her eyes. "Yes," she said. "You're right. I've also got to go into town and arrange for a coffin. Oh, how I dread that."

"I'll do that for you," Will promised.

"Oh, would you? Thank you. I can't tell you how much I appreciate not having to go through that."

Chapter Fifteen

Violetta had seen Mario and the other vaqueros when they returned to Tularosa last night. Bruised and beaten, they were barely able to sit on their horses. When someone said they had been beaten in town by gringos who worked for John Sydney Welch, she was afraid that Senor Fernandez would be so angry that he would lead his men in an attack against the Red Rock. But when Fernandez found out the entire story, how Senor Crockett had been tricked, then tied and beaten by four of his own men, he grew very angry.

"Why would you do such a thing?" he asked.

"*Mi patron,* we did it for you," Mario tried to explain. "These hombres, Will Crockett and his *hermano,* are *pistoleros* for Senor Welch. We thought to make sure that their pistols would not be used against Rancho Tularosa."

"Senor Welch is not our enemy," Fernandez said.

"But such things as this could make him our enemy. I must now go to him and apologize. And though it is an act of humiliation, I will do it, for it is something that must be done."

"I'm sorry, senor, I thought you would be pleased with this."

"Pleased? How can I be pleased? We are men of honor," Fernandez said. "Mario, I am from a long line of noblemen, going back to the days when my ancestors were honored by the king of Spain for their bravery. I will not have my ancestors dishonored by dishonorable men!"

Fernandez's angry shouts could be heard all over the hacienda, and the servants of the house moved quickly and quietly to avoid his ire.

But then, suddenly, the shouting and angry words stopped. For the next several moments, there were only subdued voices. Then a whispered rumor began working its way through Rancho Tularosa, whispered by coachman to maid, by maid to cook, by cook to stable man, by stable man to vaquero until, within moments, everyone knew.

Senor John Sydney Welch was dead, shot down in a saloon in Riata.

"Now there will be great trouble," Fernandez said. "The entire population of Riata is Mexican. I fear that the people who are left at the Red Rock will join forces with High Point Ranch. The war that I did not want is about to be forced upon us."

It was late, and the house was very quiet. Violetta was certain that by now everyone was asleep. That was good. It was necessary that everyone be asleep in order for her to carry out her plan.

Quietly, she got out of bed and began dressing.

Don Fernandez's words, "The war that I did not want is about to be forced upon us," burned into her heart. Surely, such a thing could be avoided if only reason were applied. Someone should do something to stop this before it went any further.

But who was that someone?

She was that someone, Violetta decided.

And why not? Had not she and Caroline Welch become fast friends? And with Senor Welch dead, then his daughter would be in charge of the ranch, and surely her words would be listened to.

Violetta would go to Caroline Welch and offer her condolences on the death of her father. She was sure that the mood at Tularosa was such that no one else would do it. Besides, such a visit would also give her the opportunity to beg her friend Caroline to work for peace, if not between Tularosa and High Point, then at least between Tularosa and the Red Rock.

Dressed now, Violetta stepped out of her room and into the long hall. The hallway was thickly carpeted, and the carpet's rich texture cradled her feet as she walked silently down the length of the corridor. She could hear snoring and soft, measured breathing coming from the other rooms.

The house was dark, but a splash of moonlight coming in through a front window guided her down the stairs. When she reached the bottom of the stairs, she was startled by a sudden clicking noise, followed by a whirring sound.

Dong!

It was the hall clock, announcing the time.

Quietly, Violetta let herself out of the house. She went out to the tack room, selected her saddle, then mounted and rode away quietly, without being seen.

Half an hour later, on the road to the Red Rock Ranch, her horse suddenly started favoring its right foreleg.

"Oh, Diablo, what is wrong?" she asked, dismounting and running her hand up and down the animal's leg. The horse flinched at her touch.

For some reason that he couldn't figure out, Quinn Turner always had an overpowering need for a woman after he killed someone. But this time, it wasn't just any woman. Seeing all those Mexican women in Riata, their golden skin, the long black hair and flashing black eyes, had given him a desire for someone like that. So, after returning from Riata, he went to the Mexican cantina.

Although the cantina was still buzzing with the excitement of the incident involving Will and Gid Crockett, it had returned to "business as usual". Turner ordered a tequila and expressed his intent to buy Lola's services. Then he sat in the corner of the cantina and waited.

He waited until after midnight, cursing under his breath at whoever was taking up so much of her time upstairs. While he waited, he continued to drink tequila, and he was about half-drunk when he learned that Lola wasn't here at all. She had slipped out the back way at about eleven-thirty.

"What the hell did she do that for?" Turner demanded. "She knew I was waiting for her!"

"I do not know, Senor Turner. Perhaps she forgot," the bartender said, although the bartender knew full well that Lola hadn't forgotten but had sneaked out the back way *because* Turner was here.

Drunk, frustrated, and angry, Turner had mounted his horse and was now riding toward High Point. The road to High Point ran west, from Carmen. Four miles outside of Carmen, a road branched off to the south. This was the road to Tularosa. A little over a mile later, another road branched off to the north, this one going to the Red Rock Ranch.

High Point was straight ahead on the road, due west.

Turner was on that stretch of road between the two junctions to Tularosa and Red Rock when he saw a horse. At first, he thought the horse was alone. Then he saw that someone was standing alongside it, examining its leg. He saw too that the person was a young woman...a young *Mexican* woman.

"Lola!" he said under his breath. He slapped his legs against the side of his horse, urging it into a lope. The girl didn't hear him until the last moment, then she looked up, startled that someone would be out here at this time.

When she looked up, Turner saw that it wasn't Lola but was instead the young girl who had come to marry Alfredo. He smiled broadly. Hell, this was even *better* than running across Lola. He dismounted.

"Having a problem?" he asked.

"Si, senor. My horse, he is hurt. I think I cannot ride him now without hurting him more."

Turner bent down to touch the horse's leg, and again the horse flinched.

"Yeah, he's gone lame all right," Turner said, standing up. He ran the back of his hand across his mouth as he looked at the young girl, standing in the moonlight. She was much prettier than Lola. "Tell me, what's a pretty little thing like you doin' out here on the road at this time of night?"

"I am going to visit my friend Senorita Caroline at the Red Rock Ranch," Violetta said.

"She must be a pretty good friend to let you come wake her up in the middle of the night like this."

"Si, senor. We are very good friends, but I think she may not be sleeping this night. There is much sorrow over there now. Perhaps you have not heard. Her father has been killed."

"Oh, yes, I know all about it," Turner said. "I'm the one who kilt him." He smiled again, and Violetta thought she had never seen evil more personified than in the countenance of this man.

"You! You killed him, senor?"

"I did."

"But why? Why would you do such a thing?"

"Hell, girly, I did it because I wanted to," Turner said. He started unbuckling his belt. "Now there's something else I wanna do."

"Senor, no, please," Violetta said in a quiet, pleading voice.

"You're just playin' shy," Turner said. "You know you really like what a real man can do for you. All you Mex girls like it."

Violetta turned and tried to run, but she was blocked on one side by her horse, and on the other by Turner, so that she had nowhere to go. As a result, Turner caught her easily, then threw her to the ground.

When Turner finished, he stood up and looked down at the young girl, whimpering in the dirt, her dress torn and bloodied.

"All right, girly, that was good," he said gruffly. "Now get up."

Violetta lay there, sobbing quietly.

"I said, get up," he repeated. He leaned down and grabbed one of her arms and started pulling her up. "You wasn't hurt none."

Suddenly, and unexpectedly, the young girl, with amazingly quick reflexes, grabbed Turner's pistol and pulled it from his holster.

"What the hell?" Turner shouted aloud, backing away from her quickly. If he hadn't been half-drunk, and if he hadn't been caught totally by surprise, she never would have managed to get his gun. But have it she did, and Turner, feeling absolute panic welling up inside of him, held both hands out in front of him, as if by that action to push her away.

"What are you goin' to do?" he asked in fear. "Girly, I was just funnin' with you! You know that."

Violetta, her eyes wide and wild-looking, pointed the pistol toward him. The barrel was wavering.

"Woman, put that gun down! It's liable to go off!"

Then, in a move that was as unexpected as the move which had secured the pistol for her in the first place, Violetta turned the gun toward herself. Pushing the barrel in between her breasts, still exposed because he had ripped away her dress, she pulled the trigger.

"What the—" Turner shouted over the sound of the shot as he saw Violetta go down with blood pumping from the large wound in her chest. She fell flat on her back in the road with her arms spread out on either side. The pistol, a little wisp of smoke still curling up from the end of the barrel, was lying right beside her.

Quickly, Turner picked up the pistol and held it for a moment, as if somehow this young, mortally wounded girl might rise up and attack him. Turner had been in many gunfights, and he had almost lost count of the number of men he had killed, but never, after any of them, had he experienced the same sort of disquiet he was feeling now.

"What the hell did you do that for, you crazy bitch?" he asked.

He looked down at her for a full moment longer, then, convinced that she was dead, he walked slowly back to his horse, mounted it, and continued his ride to High Point Ranch.

Chapter Sixteen

Carmen

When Will Crockett rode into Carmen the next morning, the whole town was talking about the body of the young Mexican girl that had been found on the road.

She had been brought into town, but already Don Fernandez and four of his men had come for her. They put her body in the back of a wagon, covered her with a tarpaulin, and were about to start back out to Tularosa when Fernandez saw Will. He rode over to him.

"You have heard, senor? About the young senorita who would have become my sister-in-law?"

"Yes, Don Fernandez," Will said. "I just heard. I'm very sorry."

"Who could do such a thing?" Fernandez asked. "She was so young, and beautiful."

"I hope you don't think it was anyone from Red

Rock," Will said.

Fernandez shook his head. "No, I do not think that. I think she was attacked, on the road, by someone who is not a man but is a monster. What I do not know is why she was on the road at night, so far from the *hacienda*."

With a sad shake of his head, Fernandez turned his head and looked back toward the wagon which, by now, was at the far end of the street. "To be raped and murdered like that?" He shook his head. "This has nothing to do with a range war, senor. This is the act of someone who is truly evil."

"I agree, Don Fernandez," Will said.

Fernandez sighed. "I know that Violetta was fond of Senorita Welch. Would you tell her for me what happened? Such news, though distressing, cannot be as bad as the loss she is already suffering."

"I'll tell her," Will promised.

"Muchas gracias."

Fernandez touched his hand to the brim of his large, silver-embroidered sombrero, then turned his horse and urged it into a brief gallop in order to enable him to catch up with the others.

As Will watched Fernandez ride away, he happened to see Quinn Turner standing just outside the saloon door. Turner didn't see him, because he was staring intently at the wagon bearing Violetta's body out of town.

At that instant, almost as if he had received some sort of spiritual enlightenment, Will knew that Quinn Turner was the one who had killed Violetta.

"You son of a bitch!" Will swore under his breath. "In the last two days you have killed John Sydney Welch and Violetta Martinez. Mister Turner, you've got a lot to answer for."

Half an hour later, Will was in the back of the general store, looking over the supply of coffins.

"Can you believe Fernandez didn't even buy a coffin? He claims he has carpenters on the ranch, and they'll build a coffin for that girl. But, of course," Campbell said, dismissing the whole thing with a shrug of his shoulders, "they are Mexicans. And ever'one knows that Mexicans do things different. Now, Mister Crockett, what can I do for you?"

"I'm here to buy a coffin for Miss Welch," Will said.

Campbell, who had been visibly disappointed over losing a sale to Fernandez, now brightened.

"Ah, yes!" he said. "Yes, indeed." He assumed a practiced look of sorrow. "I was much distressed to hear of Mister Welch's demise. He was one of our community's finest citizens. And as such, he deserves the finest coffin modern science can offer."

"What do you have?" Will asked.

The confident smile of a salesman returned. "Well,

this is a particularly nice one," the store owner said. "It is said that this is the same style coffin used to bury Abraham Lincoln." Andrew Campbell was, in addition to the undertaker, storekeeper for the general store, and he proudly displayed a sign in front of his store which read: *Andrew Campbell Mercantile and Undertaking Service, providing for all mankind, from the cradle to the grave.*

"Saying they used it to bury Lincoln doesn't make that much of an impression on me," Will replied. "I fought with the South."

"Yes, to be sure, as did most of us here," Campbell ad-libbed quickly in order that his faux pas not lose him the sale.

"But the coffin looks all right," Will continued.

"Oh, Mister Crockett, it is far better than 'all right'," Campbell insisted. "This is our very best model, and as you can see, it is really quite beautiful."

The coffin had a highly polished black finish, trimmed in silver, and lined with red satin.

"It's very popular with the womenfolk. And I believe you did say you were making the coffin selection for Miss Welch?"

"Yes."

Will ran his hand over the surface. The finish was as smooth as silk and the gloss was such that he could see his reflection in it.

"This is called the Eternal Cloud, and it is guaranteed for one hundred years," Campbell explained, continuing his sales pitch.

Will cocked his head and looked at Campbell. "One hundred years?"

"Yes, sir. One hundred years."

"What then?"

"I beg your pardon?"

"What happens after one hundred years if the coffin hasn't held up? Who will be here to redeem it?"

For a moment Campbell was confused, then, seeing the logic, or perhaps, the illogic of it, he chuckled. "Yes," he said. "I believe you are right. But take my word for it. It is a good coffin."

"Very well, I'll take it. Have it sent out to Red Rock."

"Yes, sir," Campbell agreed. "I'll have it there this afternoon."

Will started to leave, then looking through the window, across the street, he saw Turner just going back into the Americana Saloon.

He felt a sense of barely controlled anger build up inside him, and when he looked back inside, he saw a plain, pine box. It too was a coffin, though it was as plain a coffin as Will had ever seen.

"How much is that one?" he asked, pointing to the pine box coffin.

"Oh, sir, you wouldn't want anything like that connected with Mister Welch's funeral," Campbell gasped in horror. "Why, that is the kind of coffin the territorial government uses to bury prisoners who have been hanged."

"The casket is not for Mister Welch," Will said easily. And then he asked, "How much?"

"Five dollars," Campbell said.

Will took five dollars from his pocket. "I'll take it."

"You mean, in addition to the one you have just bought for Mister Welch?" Campbell asked, anxious to make certain that he hadn't lost the previous and much more lucrative sale.

"Yes."

"Very good, sir. And what would you have me do with it?"

"You have ink and paper?"

"Yes, of course I do."

"I want to make a sign, then I'll tell you where to put the coffin."

"Yes, sir."

Campbell found Will a large piece of paper, a bottle of ink, and a wide-quill pen. Will got busy, and a few minutes later, finished with his sign.

"I want you to put that coffin in the front window of your store," Will said. "And I want you to attach this sign to the coffin."

Campbell looked at the sign, then blanched visibly. "Oh, uh, sir, are you sure you want me to use this sign?"

"I am absolutely sure," Will said. "Now, put the pine box in the window and attach this sign to it, like I told you to."

"Yes, sir," Campbell said.

Since John Sydney Welch wasn't a man who often went to church, Caroline thought that a church funeral would be inappropriate. However, she did ask the town's only Protestant parson to conduct the service, and he agreed.

The funeral was held at the Red Rock Ranch, and three fourths of the town showed up to pay their respects. Many of the cowboys who now worked for Broomfield also showed up. Several of them had worked for John Sydney in the past, and even those who hadn't worked for him knew him by reputation to be a good man who was fair to his hands.

"Miss Caroline, if you'd like a hard-workin' hand, I'd be more'n proud to come work for you," Silas Woodruff said. Caroline remembered Silas as a young man who had worked for her father in the past but had gone over to High Point, when Broomfield promised more money.

"Silas, I appreciate it, I really do," Caroline replied. "But the truth is, my father ran the business. I don't know whether we need another hand, whether we can afford you, or even if we can afford the hands we have now."

"You can afford me all right," Silas said. "'Cause I'll work for nothin' if need be. I can't see myself workin' for Broomfield no more. Not after he stood by and watched Turner gun down your pa like he done."

Caroline gasped. "What do you mean, he stood by? Do you mean to tell me that Broomfield was there?"

"Yes, ma'am, he was there all right. And the word I got is, he didn't do nothin' a'tall to try and stop the fight from a-happenin'."

Caroline reached out to touch Silas on the arm. "Thank you, Silas," she said. "And of course you can come work on the ranch. I'll talk to Marcellus. We'll pay you the same as we're paying the others, for as long as we have any money to pay anyone."

It wasn't long after her conversation with Silas that Broomfield showed up, arriving in a highly polished black carriage pulled by a team of matching grays. Silas's story had spread quickly through all the cowboys, and many of them turned their backs, almost pointedly, as Broomfield passed through them. Broomfield sought out Caroline to personally extend his sympathy.

"Mister Broomfield," Caroline said, getting right to the point. "I have been told that you were there, that you saw my father killed."

Broomfield cleared his throat. "Yes," he said. "I was

there."

"Why haven't you come over before now? Why didn't you come to me right after it happened?"

"I figured you needed some time to mourn," Broomfield replied. "Besides, what I would have to tell you about your pa would only hurt you more. Didn't see much need in hurting you any more than you were already hurting."

"What do you mean? How could what you have to tell me, possibly hurt me more than I am already hurting? My father is dead, Mister Broomfield. What pain is left?"

"The way he died," Broomfield said. "The foolishness of it. His *own* foolishness," he added.

"Please, tell me how. And tell me how it was that you happened to be there."

"I had gone down to Riata to see General Berto Bolanos."

"The outlaw?"

"The *revolucionario,*" Broomfield said. "I will admit that Bolanos has the reputation of being a *bandido,* but what he really is, Miss Welch, is a hero to his people. He is fighting a war against a very unpopular government, not unlike our own Civil War not too many years ago. I am proud to say, by the way, that I fought for the Confederacy during that war. And just as I fought against an oppressive government then, so too is Bolanos fighting an oppressive government now."

"Yes, but my father was no revolutionary. What does all that have to do with him? And why was he there?"

"I'm getting to that," Broomfield said. "I went to see Bolanos to see if he would act as an intermediary in my fight with Fernandez. I want this foolish war between us to end, and I thought that Bolanos, being both a Mexican and a hero to his people, might be able to work something out." Broomfield paused for a moment.

"Go on," Caroline said.

"Well, your pa showed up. I didn't even know he was there. One minute, Bolanos and I were discussing how best to make peace, and the next minute your pa was there, making accusations that Bolanos and I were teaming up. He started talking crazy talk, saying wild things."

"So you had Turner shoot him?"

"No!" Broomfield said quickly. "No, it wasn't like that. I just asked Turner to show your pa outside. Bolanos and I were engaged in a private conversation and things had reached a delicate stage. The ranting and raving of your father could have ruined it."

"How did it go from 'showing my father outside' to shooting him?"

"Turner didn't shoot your father down in cold blood, Miss Welch. It was a fair gunfight."

"A *fair* gunfight? What could be fair about it? In the first place, I was told that my father didn't even have a gun with him. And in the second place, what on earth would cause him to get into a gunfight with a known gunfighter? My father was no coward, Mister Broomfield, but he was no fool, either. He was a sensible man, and sensible men do not go around issuing challenges to professional gunfighters."

"Who knows what goes through the mind of a proud man who believes he has been wronged? I tried to get your father to get on his horse and leave. I hoped he would do so, then return when tempers were cooled. When I saw that he wouldn't do that, I did the only thing I could think of. I furnished your father with a gun."

"You? You gave him the gun he used?"

"I am proud to say that I did."

"But why? If he hadn't had a gun, he couldn't have had the fight."

"Miss Welch, I know that your father and I didn't always see eye to eye on business, but I had a great deal of respect for him. I couldn't stand by and watch him get shot down in cold blood. I figured he ought to at least have the chance to defend himself. I mean, you understand that, don't you?"

"I...I don't know," Caroline said. She had to admit that, in a terrible, tragic way, everything Broomfield was saying to her made sense.

"One final thing," Broomfield continued. "Now that

your pa is gone, I know that it will be very difficult—if not impossible—for you to continue to run this ranch. I would be honored to take over the operation of the ranch for you."

"What do you mean?" Caroline asked.

"I would manage it, so to speak. Join your cowboys with mine, join your herd with mine, and run it all as one ranch. That way you would still have the benefits of a ranch, without the headache of running one. Or, of course, if you prefer, I could just buy the ranch from you. I wouldn't be able to pay top dollar right now, you understand. I'm a little short of cash because of several recent business deals. But I assure you, it would be enough money to make your life quite comfortable."

"Thank you, Mister Broomfield," Caroline said. "I will think about it."

"Miss Welch," the preacher said, coming over to her then. "If you are ready, we'll start with the service now."

After the funeral, Caroline stood at her father's graveside for a long time, even after the others had gone, and looked at the pile of dirt that the grave diggers were throwing down on the "Eternal Cloud" coffin.

She had wept bitter tears of grief when she'd first learned the news, but now her eyes were dry, and her sorrow was numbed. There remained only anger at the brutal and senseless killing. Finally, she left the cemetery.

She would have to put the sorrow behind her. She had a ranch to run, and her "people" to look out for. She had thought about Broomfield's offer, just as she'd said she would, and now she had made a decision.

Caroline was not going to let him manage the ranch, and she was not going to sell to him. Her father had spent half a lifetime building Red Rock Ranch, and she was not going to let him down. She would run it herself. She knew that it was what her father would want.

Chapter Seventeen

Immediately after the funeral, Will rode into town to see if Campbell had followed his instructions. It wasn't long after he arrived in the saloon that he knew Campbell had done what Will had asked of him. He knew it from the buzz of curious questioning that was going on among the customers. They moved from bar to table, and from table to table, to whisper the news.

"Have you seen it? Have you looked in Campbell's window?"

"Can you believe Campbell putting something up like that?"

"You can bet your last dollar Campbell didn't do somethin' like that on his own."

"All hell's goin' to break loose. That's all I got to say about it. All hell's goin' to break loose."

Only Turner, the small, evil-tempered gunman who

worked for Broomfield, seemed to be left out of the conversation. At first, he was busy with a game of solitaire and he didn't even notice he was being systematically left out. Then the piano stopped playing and gradually all conversation quieted to a hushed whisper. It wasn't until then, until it was so quiet you could hear a pin drop, that Turner, curious about the sudden cessation of noise, happened to glance up. He saw that everyone was staring at him.

"What is it?" he asked in an irritated voice. "What's ever'body so quiet for? What the hell are you all lookin' at?"

"Nothing," someone mumbled.

"If there ain't nothin', why are you all lookin' at me?"

"We was wonderin' if you'd seen the coffin over to Campbell's store? And the sign he put up in it?" one brave soul asked.

"What coffin? What sign?"

Silently, one of the men pointed outside. "It's not somethin' you tell about, it's somethin' you got to see," he said. "It's across the street, in Campbell's store."

"All this whisperin' and carryin' on is about a coffin? What the hell do I care about a coffin?"

"You might be interested in this particular coffin, Mister Turner."

"Why would I be?"

Although everyone continued to stare nervously at

Turner, none of them were willing to provide him with the answer he was looking for.

"All right, if none of you is man enough to tell me what this is all about, I'll just go see for myself," Turner said gruffly. He got up and walked over to the batwing doors where he stood for a moment looking down the street toward Campbell's General Store. A crowd of curious onlookers had gathered on the porch and in the street in front of the store. The crowd was growing larger, even as Turner stood there looking at it.

Because of the size of the crowd, Turner couldn't see what they were looking at in the window.

"What the hell?" he said irritably. "How can a body see anythin' with all those people standin' there?"

He pushed through the doors, then started across the street.

"Here he comes!" someone said.

"Get out of the way! Let him through!"

"You all right, Mister Turner?"

"Damn right, I'm all right. Why shouldn't I be?" Turner replied. "What's goin' on here?"

No one answered, but they did open up a path so he could step up onto the porch and look into Campbell's front window.

That was when he saw the object of everyone's attention, an open pine coffin. Turner stared in disbelief, not only at the coffin, but at a hand-painted sign:

THIS COFFIN RESERVED FOR QUINN TURNER

Turner pointed at the sign.

"Campbell, get out here!" he screamed in choked anger. "You son of a bitch! I'll kill you for this!"

"Andrew Campbell didn't do this, Turner. I did," a quiet voice from the crowd said.

Turner whirled around at the sound of the voice, and the crowd scattered, leaving only one person behind.

There, standing in the middle of the street calmly, almost casually, was Will Crockett.

"Are you crazy, mister?" Turner asked. "Are you lookin' to get yourself kilt?"

"No, Turner," Will replied. "What I'm looking for is a reason to kill you."

Turner smiled, a slow, evil smile. "And have you come up with a reason to kill me?" he asked.

Will shook his head. "I'm afraid I haven't," he answered.

"Well, now, I'm just real glad you couldn't come up with a reason to kill me. For a moment there, you had me just really scared," Turner said in a sarcastic tone of voice.

"I couldn't come up with a *reason,*" Will continued, "so I decided I'm just going to have to kill you for the hell of it."

The evil smile froze on Turner's face. Turner wasn't used to this kind of reaction from men he faced. Normally the reaction was one of fear, bordering on panic. And it was the terror that he engendered that tended to skew the gunfights to his side.

The intimidation of his opponent was all a part of Turner's strategy. He figured that it normally took his adversary at least half a second to overcome his numbing fear and start his draw. That half a second was all the edge Turner needed.

But he wasn't going to realize that edge with this man. He had never seen anyone as calm as Will Crockett was at this moment. And, oddly, Will's demeanor was beginning to have the same effect on Turner that Turner's cold calculation normally had on the people that he faced.

Turner tried to push the gnawing little worm of fear back, and he forced an evil grin, intending to regain some of the edge he had given up.

"I'm goin' to enjoy this," he said. "I'm goin' to kill you now, then go across the street and have me a good supper."

"It's too late for supper, Turner," Will said. "The next meal you eat will be breakfast. And you'll be eating that in hell."

Suddenly Turner made the move for his gun. He was fast, so fast that, for a split second, Will wondered if, perhaps, he might have made a mistake. But such thoughts, as fleeting as they were, had no bearing on the situation now. Both men were committed to the deadly game, and only one would survive this confrontation.

Will beat Turner by a fraction of a second. He fired, his bullet catching Turner in the chest. But Turner had already sent the signal to his trigger finger so, as he spun around, his finger, reacting too late, pulled the trigger. The bullet plunked into the side of a watering trough as Turner fell face down in a freshly-deposited horse apple. A stream of water arced out from the bullet hole, splashing on the back of Turner's neck and making brown-green tributaries of horse manure as it ran in rivulets out into the street. He didn't make another move.

The display in the front of Campbell's store became even more bizarre after Turner was killed. What had been an empty coffin with a sign was now a filled coffin. Turner was placed in the coffin with his hands folded across his chest. In his right hand was his pistol. In his left was a knife. His left eye was closed, his right eye half-open. His yellowed, crooked teeth were disclosed because of the missing lip. He was wearing the same thing he had on when he was shot.

The coffin was standing upright so everyone could see its contents, quite clearly. Someone, remembering that Turner had been playing a game of solitaire just before he was killed, slipped that same deck of cards into his shirt pocket.

"That way, the son of a bitch can play cards in hell," he said.

Those who were gathered around laughed.

Across the street from Campbell's, in the Americana Saloon, the conversation was spirited and the mood upbeat. Though it was only mid-afternoon, the saloon was as full as it normally was at night. The piano player was kept busy with requests for cheery songs, and loud, masculine guffaws and the high, piercing laughter of women turned the saloon into a cacophony of song and frolic.

Although no one actually said so, the ebullient mood was directly related to Turner's being killed. He was unliked in life, and unlamented in death.

The closest anyone came to actually mourning Turner's passing was the foul mood of B. J. Broomfield. Broomfield was sitting at a table in the back of the saloon, drinking whiskey and staring morosely into his glass. Katie Ann was sitting at the table with him.

"Who would have thought Will Crockett could beat Turner?" Broomfield asked.

"I guess Will thought he could," Katie Ann replied.

"I suppose you're happy about the way the fight turned out," Broomfield snarled.

"Are you asking if I'm happy Will killed Turner, instead of the other way around? Of course, I'm happy."

"You should've told me that you knew the Crocketts

from before the war."

"The subject never came up."

"It's come up now, though, hasn't it? How many times have you been with Gid Crockett since they got here?"

In fact, Katie Ann had not been with Gid at all, at least not in the way Broomfield meant. But she thought of Gid, and the sweet agony seeing him again had caused.

"I don't know," Katie Ann replied. "Anyway, why should it bother you? I've been a working girl, you know that. I've been with lots of men."

"Yes, but I'll bet you haven't been with any of 'em the same way you've been with Gid Crockett. You haven't even been with me the way you have been with Gid Crockett."

"It's my job."

"No. When you're with Gid Crockett, it's more than a job. You like it too much."

"Whether or not I like Gid Crockett has nothing at all to do with my being glad that his brother killed Turner. It wouldn't matter who killed Turner, I would feel the same way. And, surely, you can't say that you actually liked that evil little man?"

"Like him?" Broomfield replied. "No, I didn't like the son of a bitch."

"Then why are you sitting here with such a sour expression on your face?"

"Because when you do business the way I do business, you need a Turner," Broomfield answered. "He was a useful tool. Now that tool is gone, and I have no one to replace him."

"What kind of tool could someone like Turner be?" Katie Ann asked.

"He was a fast gun," Broomfield answered. "Only it turns out that Will Crockett was faster. Funny, I knew Crockett during the war, saw him in battle many times, and never knew that he was that fast."

"I wouldn't think being fast would necessarily be a requirement for a soldier," Katie Ann suggested. "I mean, it's just a matter of fighting and killing, isn't it? You don't move out into the middle of the battlefield and challenge the enemy to draw, do you?"

Broomfield looked at Katie Ann with a strange expression on his face. "No," he said. "You don't." He stood up and looked down at her. "Let's go upstairs."

"I beg your pardon?"

"I said, let's go upstairs."

"Now? It's the middle of the afternoon," Katie Ann said.

"So, what does that matter? We've done it in the daytime before."

"But, not now...not after all that's happened."

"What has happened that would have anything to do with whether or not we go upstairs?"

"You know what I'm talking about. First Mister Welch was killed, then that poor little Mexican girl. And now Turner."

"I don't see that that has anything to do with anything," Broomfield said. "I didn't like Welch or Turner in the first place. And the girl? Hell, she's just another Mexican as far as I'm concerned, and there isn't much difference between them and Indians. It's no loss when one of them is killed, be they man or woman."

"I don't feel that way. A human life is a human life. And I don't think it would be proper for us to go upstairs."

"You don't give any more of a damn about Welch or Turner than I do," Broomfield said. "And you're just using the Mexican girl as an excuse. You don't want me with you, because you've got Gid Crockett on your mind all the time."

"All right, I'll admit it, he is on my mind," Katie said. "And if you're honest with yourself, you'll have to admit that he's on your mind too. You know that I want him and not you."

Broomfield snorted. "What the hell are you talking about? I don't give a damn what you want. I provide a place for you to stay and I let you earn a living. And what do I get out of this? I get me a piece of ass anytime I want it, and that time is now. I said get up to that room, now."

"No."

"What do you mean, no?" Broomfield asked coldly. "You can't say no to me."

"I've got the right to say no to anyone I want."

Broomfield leaned over the table and put his hand to her neck. She felt something sharp pressing against her skin and she gasped.

"That's right, Cat Clay. It's a knife," he said. "One twitch of my hand and I'll cut your jugular open. You'll bleed to death in less than a minute."

"You wouldn't dare."

"You don't know me, little missy. After you're dead I'll give you a big funeral and tell everyone how much I'm going to miss you. And don't think the fact that you're a woman will stop me from killing you. I killed plenty of women in my time." He smiled evilly.

"I...I believe you would at that," Katie Ann said.

"Now, let's get upstairs," Broomfield said as he yanked her off the chair.

Chapter Eighteen

"Don't bother with any of the niceties," Broomfield said gruffly when he pushed Katie Ann into her room. He grabbed her and threw her down on the bed.

"You don't have to do this," she protested.

"Shut up!" Broomfield said, slapping her savagely, as he ripped her dress down the front.

"Ow! Why are you—"

"I said, shut up!" Broomfield said, slapping her again—harder this time than before.

She had been "on the line" for a long time now and had been with more men than she could count. Some had been gentle, and others not, but never had she been treated as savagely as this.

When it was over Broomfield stood by the side of the bed, looking down at her used body, exposed by the torn dress. He rebuttoned his pants.

"Damn," he said. "That's the best you've ever put out."

"You didn't have to do it that way," Katie said in a voice barely above a whisper.

"Don't you say a damn word. I gave you your chance, and you told me no. Well, I got news for you, missy. You're a hell of a lot *better* this way." There was a demonic gleam in his eyes. "And this is the way we're goin' to do it every time from now on."

Katie Ann raised her right arm and, crooked at the elbow, lay the forearm across her eyes. She made no effort to shield her exposed body from his gaze. Instead, she chose not to look at him.

"You said something downstairs that I've been thinking about," Broomfield said as he continued to straighten his clothes.

"What is that?" Katie asked softly. Her arm was still over her eyes.

"War."

"War?"

"You said, in a war it doesn't matter whether someone is fast with a gun or not. Funny you would have to point that out to me, seein' as I've been in a war and you haven't."

Katie Ann said nothing.

"So, I figure the best way to beat someone who is really fast with a pistol is to get them in a war."

"You aren't making one bit of sense. There isn't any

war."

"Not yet," Broomfield said. "But I've got at least a hundred men working for me at High Point. And they'll do anything I tell them to if I pay 'm enough. To a man, they fought in the War of Aggression, and they're all ready to get mighty aggressive right now. First thing I'm going to do is clear out what's left of the Red Rock, including your beloved, Gid Crockett. After that, I'm going to take on Tularosa and get rid of a bunch of damned Mexicans."

Now Katie Ann lowered her arm and stared at him with a horrified expression on her face. "You don't mean that. If you do that, you'll cause a bloodbath."

"Well, that's the way it is when you fight a war," Broomfield said. He opened the door, but before he left, he turned back toward the bed and smiled. Somehow, the smile was even more frightening than his words had been. "It's going to be good between you and me from now on," he said. "You just get used to it."

He left, slamming the door behind him, and Katie Ann lay on the bed, shaking from humiliation and fright, as tears streamed down her face. She had held them back, just because she didn't want to let the bastard see her cry.

Gid Crockett had just finished washing up for supper and was reaching for the towel when he saw Katie Ann come riding up to the ranch house.

"Katie Ann!" he said, smiling broadly. "What are you doing out here?"

"Gid, you've got to warn the others. Broomfield's coming."

"Broomfield?"

"With a hundred men," she said. "He's going to make war against Red Rock Ranch!"

"One hundred men?" Marcellus gasped, when Gid took Katie Ann over to the bunkhouse to tell Will and the others of Broomfield's plan. "My God! We can never fight off a hundred men!"

"How many men do we have?" Will asked.

"No more'n ten or twelve, and that's countin' the cook," Marcellus said.

"Thirteen, counting me," a woman's voice said, and they all turned to see Caroline standing there, having been brought by curiosity when, from the house, she saw everyone gathered around the woman she knew as Cat Clay.

"Fourteen," Katie Ann said.

Marcellus rubbed his chin. "Even so, fourteen against a hundred...them sure ain't good odds. And two of ours is women."

"I can shoot a rifle, Marcellus," Caroline said. "And the bullet that comes from the end of the rifle doesn't know if it has been launched by a man or a woman. It is just as deadly."

"Yes, ma'am, you got that right," Marcellus agreed.

"Will, what about Fernandez?" Caroline asked. "If we get word to him that we are being attacked by Broomfield, maybe he will help."

"Good idea," Will said. "Silas, you want to ride over to Tularosa and tell Fernandez what's going on?"

"Wait a minute, Silas, I'll write a letter," Caroline said.

"I'll saddle my horse," Silas replied.

"You really think we can fight them off?" Marcellus asked.

"Yes, thanks to Katie Ann's warning," Will answered. He smiled at Katie Ann and Gid, who was standing with his arm around her shoulders, squeezing her affectionately.

"I don't know, if a hundred of them come…" Marcellus hedged.

"Look at it this way," Will said. "They won't come until after nightfall, and when they do come, they'll be on horseback, out in the open. We will be hidden in the dark and behind cover. Now, which would you rather be?"

"Yeah," Marcellus said. His worried expression fell away to be replaced by a smile. "Yeah, I see what you mean. They'll be sittin' ducks."

"That's the way of it."

"So, what do we do first?" Marcellus asked.

"First, we eat supper," Will replied. "No sense in trying to fight on an empty stomach."

"I was hoping you'd say that," Gid said, and the others laughed, somewhat relieving the tension of the moment.

Will ate quickly, then went outside. The sun was low in the west, giving them, by his reckoning, another hour of light. They would need the light to set up the ambush.

Gid came out after a few minutes, to stand beside him.

"How is it going in there?" Will asked.

"They're loading their rifles and pistols," Gid said. He chuckled. "You've got them about half-convinced it will be a picnic. They're actually looking forward to it."

"Well, it's not going to be quite as easy as I described," Will said. "But I had to make it sound like that, otherwise several of them might decide to leave. Then we really would be in a mess."

"They're good boys, most of them," Gid said. "I don't think they'll run out on us. Now, what do you have in mind?"

"I think we should have the men dig themselves rifle pits," Will said. "There, there, there, and there," he added, pointing out the places. "That way we'll be able to catch them in a crossfire when they arrive."

"What about blasting powder?" Gid asked. "If we could put a few bombs here and there, we might have a surprise for them."

Will nodded. "Yes, that's a real good idea. Tell you what. I'll get the men started on the rifle pits, while you and Marcellus take care of the powder. Then I'm going to find someplace where I can see who's coming. That should give us a little advanced warning."

"I could go up to Red Rock Escarpment and keep a watch," Caroline proposed. She was just returning from the house with the letter she had written to Fernandez. Silas, his horse now saddled, was leading his animal over to them, from the stable.

"No," Will said. "There's no telling when Broomfield might come. It could be just after dark, around midnight, or as late as before dawn tomorrow morning. Whoever is up there is going to have to stay awake all night."

"You don't think I can stay awake all night?"

"Maybe you can," Will agreed. "But I've done it many times before. I think it would be easier, and safer, if I did it."

"Safer? You mean for me?"

"Yes."

"If Broomfield comes over here and takes over my ranch, how safe do you think I'll be?"

"I'm not going to argue with you, Caroline," Will said.

Caroline sighed. "All right, all right, do it your way. But I would like to ride up there with you, if you don't mind."

"There's no need in—"

"Will, please?" Caroline said. "You... ou know what that place means to me. I might not get to...I mean, if things don't go well..." She let the sentence hang.

Will realized at once what she meant, and he relented. "All right," he said. "You can come up with me. But after your visit, I want you to come back down here."

"All right," she said, flashing him a large, happy smile. "And thank you."

Will rode along behind Caroline as they climbed the trail to her lookout. It only took about five minutes of easy riding, and Will figured that, in returning, he could cover the same distance in under two minutes if necessary. Once there they dismounted, and Will looked around.

Overhead, the stars glistened like diamonds on black velvet. In the distance, the Red Rock Escarpment rose in a great and mysterious dark slab of rock against the night sky. An owl landed nearby, and his wings made a soft whirr as he flew. The owl looked at Will with great, round, glowing eyes.

"I love it up here," Caroline said, her voice wistful, as if she were telling it goodbye.

"I can see why you like it," Will said. "It's a very nice place."

"It's magical," Caroline said.

A soft night breeze pushed across the glade, and Caroline shivered once as it caressed her skin. There was a scent of wildflowers on the air.

"Will, will I be able to come up here...after?" Caroline asked.

"You're asking me how the battle is going to come out."

"Yes. I suppose I am."

Will shrugged. "I was a little more positive with your men because I was building up their confidence. It probably won't be as easy as I painted it...but I do think we'll win."

Caroline laughed softly. "You aren't just trying to build up *my* confidence, are you?"

"No," Will said. He walked out to the edge of the precipice and looked in the direction of High Point. "I figure they'll come from that direction when they come, so I should see them in plenty of time to give a warning."

"Do you think Fernandez will respond to my letter?" Caroline asked. She came out to stand beside him.

"I think he will," Will said. "It would certainly be to his advantage." He turned and looked at her. "Caroline, I think it is about time you got back down there," he suggested.

"All right."

"When you get back, tell the boys not to be too trigger-happy. I don't want to get shot coming back down to warn you. And if Fernandez and his men do show up, I wouldn't want them shot either."

Caroline started to leave, then she turned back toward Will, with her eyes shining brightly.

"Oh, Will, is it evil of me? I know there is about to be a battle...but I am more excited than frightened."

Will chuckled. "If it's evil, then it is a malady that affects everyone. Men talk about how terrible war is, and there is always fear, just before a battle. But there is another side too, a darker side. There's something inside humans that makes them crave battle."

"Have you ever felt that exhilaration?"

"Of course, I have," Will admitted. "And, in a way, I suppose it isn't all that bad. It's what people draw on, to give them courage. I don't know why, but I do know it's something common in folks when danger is the greatest."

Will looked at Caroline. "Caroline?"

Will pulled her to him then, and they stood in a long silent embrace that both knew could go no further. Finally, with a reluctant sigh, Caroline pulled away from him, and the moment had passed.

"Well, all right then," she said. "I'll go down and deliver your message to the others."

Two miles away, as Silas rode at a ground-eating lope toward Tularosa, a lone rifle shot banged in the night.

Silas grabbed his chest, then tumbled back out of his saddle and fell to the road where he lay perfectly still. His horse loped on a few feet farther, then, realizing that he had lost his rider, stopped.

"*El Jefe* was right," the shooter said, reading the letter Silas was carrying. "They was fixin' to go into cahoots with Fernandez."

Chapter Nineteen

It was four o'clock in the morning before Broomfield began gathering his men for the attack on Red Rock Ranch. The night before, he had pulled them from the whorehouses and out of the saloons. Some he found passed out in the street, and one was lying half-in and half-out of a water trough.

When one of his riders brought him the letter Silas was carrying to Tularosa, Broomfield knew that his element of surprise had been compromised, probably by the slut he had just been with.

Never mind. There was more than one way to skin the cat.

"Skin the cat! That's a good one," he said, laughing to himself. "Skin the cat! That's a real good one." Especially since he planned to personally see to it that Cat Clay was skinned.

As Broomfield and his men rode through the predawn darkness toward Red Rock Ranch, he looked around at the riders who composed his army. Over the last several months he had been gathering drifters, more for their ability to fight than to work. Except for the cowboys who had come with the ranches he had taken over, no one who worked for him was worth a damn when it came to real work. Once this was all over, he planned to send them on their way. And he would be damned glad to be rid of them.

Will was on the rim of the canyon waiting for them. Years of surviving by wits and instinct had taught him the trick of being alert, even while he was asleep. He knew that staying awake the entire night would dull his edge. On the other hand, he couldn't sleep so deeply that Broomfield and his men would be able to ride in without being observed either. Therefore, he had taken a series of naps, dozing off for a few minutes, then waking up, then dozing off again.

When Broomfield's men finally did come riding up, Will awakened with a scent of danger in his nostrils and his skin tingling in anticipation. It was just before dawn, and a tiny sliver of pink stretched across the eastern horizon. He moved out onto the rim and looked down at the road. There they were, moving like shadows through the early morning darkness.

Will had left his horse saddled, and now he mounted and urged it back down the draw. He moved as quickly as he could without breaking into a gallop. A gallop, he feared, would alert Broomfield.

Gid greeted him as soon as he arrived.

"See anything?"

"They're coming," Will said calmly.

"Good. We're ready for them."

"Where are the others?"

"I've got them positioned just where you said they should be. We'll have ole Broomfield in a crossfire the moment he comes into range."

"And the powder?"

"I've got half a dozen bombs planted, with fuses laid right to my spot over there."

"Good. Set 'em off when you think they'll do the most damage."

It was light, the soft gray of early dawn, by the time Broomfield and his men came riding up, spread wide, moving slowly and quietly. They rode up close to the ranch house, then Broomfield held his hand up in a signal to halt. They stopped and stood like a row of statues, looking at the house, searching for any sign of life.

Will looked toward all the rifle pits. He saw the Red Rock people in position, waiting for the signal. He looked at the pit closest to him, then raised his finger to his lips in a sign to keep quiet, then he pointed to the next pit, indicating that the signal should be passed along.

Gid nodded and passed the signal on to Marcellus's pit, who passed it on to Caroline's pit. Everyone was absolutely quiet, totally still, as Broomfield and his men surveyed the house.

"There don't seem to be no one around," someone said. His voice carried well in the stillness of dawn, and Will and the others could hear every word.

"Maybe they hightailed it on outta here," someone else suggested.

"They didn't run," Broomfield replied. "The Crocketts rode with Quantrill. I know them well. They didn't run. You, Newt, ride up to the house and have a look around."

"All right, Boss," the man named Newt replied. He slapped his heels against the sides of his horse, then urged the animal up toward the quiet house. He cocked his rifle as he approached and held it across his saddle at the ready. He stopped about fifteen yards away from the front porch.

"Hello in there," he called. "Anyone here?"

When no one answered, Newt looked back toward Broomfield and the others. Broomfield indicated, with hand signals, that Newt should dismount and have a closer look. Newt swung down and, carrying his rifle at the ready, walked up onto the porch to knock on the door.

"Miss Welch, Miss Welch, you in there?"

When he got no answer, he walked over to the window and looked in. After that, he hopped down off the porch and walked all the way around the house, peering in every window. He reappeared from the back side.

"Ain't nobody here!" he yelled.

"Go inside. Make sure," Broomfield ordered.

Newt leaned his rifle against the wall of the house and pulled his pistol, then pushed the door open and stepped inside. Broomfield and the others waited quietly for a few moments. Soon, Newt reappeared, waving both arms.

"What do we do now, Boss?" one of the men asked. "You want to burn the place down?"

"Hell no! I aim to move in here when this is over. I sure as hell don't want to burn it down."

Gid drew a bead on Broomfield's chest. He could drop him now, and Broomfield would never know what hit him. It wasn't a very sporting way to kill a man.

Gid held that position for a long moment, not quite ready to kill a man from ambush. Then he recalled the war, and the battles he had been in. He had lost track of the number of men he had killed in battle, and many of them never saw the man who killed them. They had been good men too, for the most part. They were soldiers who were fighting for what they believed in. It just so happened that they had been wearing a different colored uniform, so Gid killed them.

If he could kill decent men in such a way, he certainly should have no compunctions about squeezing the trigger on this evil bastard, the one who had violated Katie Ann.

"Broomfield, most of the time when someone says, 'Go to hell', they're just saying that," Gid said under his breath. "But I'm saying it now, and that's exactly where I intend to send you." Gid squeezed the trigger.

The rifle barked and kicked back against his shoulder. He saw a puff of dust rise from Broomfield's chest, saw the bastard raise his hands in surprise, then fall off his horse.

"Son of a bitch!" someone shouted. "They're outside!"

Gid then set off a blast, and two or three of the High Point riders fell.

The firing started in general then, the High Point riders panicked by the surprise ambush and disoriented by the fact that *El Jefe* had fallen with the very first shot. In desperation, they began firing back.

Gid had spread his powder charges across the field like a fan, and as he went to work, the earth erupted in a series of horrendous explosions. Men and horses flew through the air in sickening chunks. The shock effect halted the High Point riders in their tracks, making them easy targets for the Red Rock men. They were caught in a devastating crossfire and they crumpled under the bullets, going down one by one.

Finally, Newt threw down his weapon and put up his hands.

"No! No! Don't shoot us no more! We give up! We give up!" The others followed suit so that, within a moment, every remaining High Point man had thrown down his arms and put up his hands.

"Cease fire, cease fire!" Will shouted.

As the sound of the final gunshot rolled back in an echo from the canyon walls, the smoke began drifting away. Now, after several moments of rifle fire and bomb blasts, the battlefield was quiet.

A moment later it was obvious that the quiet was deceptive, because it was broken by the sobbing and groaning of wounded men. Gradually, the defenders began coming out of their positions.

"Who's in charge here?" Will asked.

The men looked around at each other, then Newt shook his head.

"Truth to tell, mister, I don't reckon there's anyone in charge now," Newt finally said.

"Well, you seem to have more sense than most of the ones left," Will said. "I'll put you in charge."

"Yes, sir, I'll be in charge," Newt said.

"Now, would you like a little advice?"

With his hands still in the air and his eyes still wide with fright, Newt nodded.

"My advice to you is to get your wounded and your dead out of here," Will said. "Then, don't ever let me see any of you again, anywhere...ever. If you even hear my name, you'd better give me a wide berth. You got that?"

"Yes, sir," Newt answered.

"That goes for all of you," he said louder.

"Yes, sir, Mister Crockett. We ain't none of us ever goin' to cross paths with you again."

"Now get the hell out of here."

Although not one Red Rock rider was hurt during the battle, their celebration was sobered an hour later, when Fernandez personally brought Silas's body back to the ranch. Fernandez knew nothing of the morning's battle until Caroline filled him in.

"I have no idea what will happen to High Point now," Caroline said.

"I have a suggestion, senorita, if it meets with your approval."

"What is that?"

"Before evil came to our range, disguised as the man, *El Jefe*, we were a happy and productive valley. Many of the good people who owned the ranches were cheated out of them. Perhaps you and I, working together, can help those people regain their land and, once again, our valley can be a happy place."

"Oh, Senor Fernandez, I can think of nothing I would like better." She looked over at Will and smiled. "Well, perhaps one thing," she said. "But I know that it is never to be."

"Senor Fernandez," Katie Ann said then, "you don't think all of the former owners will come back, will they?"

"No, senorita, not all will come back. But we will find as many as we can and return their land to them."

"Well then, I have some money and I would like to buy some land. Perhaps a small ranch of one of the former owners who chooses not to return."

"You, senorita? A woman?"

"Why not? A woman owns Red Rock Ranch."

Fernandez smiled. *"Si,* this is true." He looked at Caroline. "Senorita Welch, do you have any objections?"

"No, none at all. I think Katie Ann would be a wonderful neighbor," Caroline said.

"Katie Ann, are you sure you want to do this?" Gid asked.

Katie put her hand on Gid's arm. "Gid, I'm not doing this for you," she said. "Whether you ever want to come back to me or not, this is what I want. I want to feel like a decent human being. And, if you ever do find yourself in this part of the country again, well, you'll have a hook for your hat...and a bed you can slide your boots under."

"Will Crockett, that goes for you as well," Caroline said. "You might like living next door to your brother."

Will and Gid looked at each other, and for a long moment, Will thought Gid might actually take Katie Ann up on her offer. In fact, if he admitted it to himself, Caroline's offer held a strong appeal for him as well. Finally, he looked back at Caroline and Katie Ann. They had noticed the glance exchanged by the two brothers, and for a fleeting moment held on to what had seemed an irrational hope.

Then they saw the look in Will's and Gid's eyes, and they knew that they had lost their bid.

"I'm not going to say yes," Will said. "And I'm not going to say no."

Caroline's eyebrows raised in question. "Then, what are you going to say?" she asked.

"I'm going to say, not yet."

Katie Ann looked quickly at Gid.

"I'll go along with that," Gid said.

"Good enough, I reckon," Katie Ann said. She smiled, then stepped up to Gid and kissed him.

"And *I'll* go along with *that,"* Caroline added, and, like Katie Ann, she stepped up to kiss Will, doing so to the accompaniment of a few good-natured whistles and catcalls from the cowboys.

The two brothers rode away from the ranch, saying nothing to each other for nearly an hour. When the rain came up, they pulled out their slickers and hunkered down inside them, riding on, lost in their own private thoughts.

With no sense of destination or purpose, Will turned north.

Gid went with him.

A Look At: Judgment Day
(The Crocketts' Western Saga: Seven)

A five-star masterpiece from best-selling author Robert Vaughan.

Will and Gid are looking forward to a quiet rest in the tiny town of Sulphur Springs. But Will's female companion offers more than he bargained for when she says her brother was murdered by outlaws. It's more than the marshal can handle, but word is that the Crockett brothers can.

AVAILABLE NOVEMBER 2021

About the Author

Robert Vaughan sold his first book when he was 19. That was 57 years and nearly 500 books ago. He wrote the novelization for the mini-series Andersonville. Vaughan wrote, produced, and appeared in the History Channel documentary Vietnam Homecoming.

His books have hit the NYT bestseller list seven times. He has won the Spur Award, the PORGIE Award (Best Paperback Original), the Western Fictioneers Lifetime Achievement Award, received the Readwest President's Award for Excellence in Western Fiction, is a member of the American Writers Hall of Fame and is a Pulitzer Prize nominee.

Vaughan is also a retired army officer, helicopter pilot with three tours in Vietnam. And received the Distinguished Flying Cross, the Purple Heart, The Bronze Star with three oak leaf clusters, the Air Medal for valor with 35 oak leaf clusters, the Army Commendation Medal, the Meritorious Service Medal, and the Vietnamese Cross of Gallantry.

Made in the USA
Coppell, TX
15 July 2022